Princess

A
Novel
By

Rukyyah J. Karreem

Erotic Ink Publishing

The characters, events, and circumstances in this story are entirely fictional. Any resemblances to any person who is living or dead, place, or event are merely coincidental.

-Rukyyah J. Karreem
 Author and Publisher

Erotic Ink Publishing
www.eroticinkpublishing.com
rukyyah@eroticinkpublishing.com
eroticinkpublishing@hotmail.com
www.myspace.com/rukyyah
www.myspace.com/eroticinkpublishing
Copyright © 2008 by Rukyyah J. Karreem
All rights Reserved
ISBN 978-0-9796297-1-6

Dedications:

This book is dedicated to Kylea J. Jones, you are the reason I strive for success. Mommy loves you with all of my heart.

This book is also dedicated to all the Princesses from Annapolis, Maryland.

Thank You

First and foremost, I like to thank God for blessing me yet again.

To my big sister, Ayesha Karreem, love you for everything.

My sister and brother, Ramona and Charles Gray Jr., love you much.

My family Samantha Elliott, Yolanda Jefferies, LaTanya Barnes, Tina Barnes, Aleasha Arnold, Crystal Arnold, Raymond Henson, Lamont Henson, Brandy Arnold, and Unika Galloway, love you all.

My niece, Jaterra Gray, I love you.

All my little cousins, Love you!

To all my close friends, Janelle Wafer, Shatema Griffin, David Henson, Yolanda Simms, Anton Jefferson, Shericka Whittington, Monique Davis, Craig Morton, and James Wyatt, love you all.

John Medley, the second author on Erotic Ink Publishing. I'm holding the door open for you to walk into your success!

To all of my author friends, Rahsaan Ali, Claudia Brown-Mosley, Rory D. Sheriff, Paula Edwards, Leila Jefferson, Shani Greene-Dowdell, and Naiomi Pitre, thank you for all of your support.

Leila Jefferson with My Time Publications, thank you for the great editing.

To my family and friends, thank you for your continued support.

If I have forgotten anyone, please forgive me and know that just because you weren't in my mind, you were still in my heart. Here is a place for you _____.

Prologue

My name is Monet Harrison but "Moni" is what they called me. I was a senior at Bowie State University and varsity cheerleader as well as a local superstar. Many chicks and some niggas hated on me too. They were jealous because the chicks wanted my man and the niggas wanted those dollars like my man had. Let's be real, money made enemies and we had a lot.

Growing up down Newtowne 20 was kind of hard for my family and me. My mother was a single mother to four children. Her job at the hospital wasn't stretching enough so public housing was the only option. I was the youngest of two older brothers and a sister. We were all really close growing up but the streets broke us up.

My brothers, Kaleo and Karreem, were hustlers. They secretly supported the family until our mother got suspicious of where the money was coming from. Not wanting drugs or dirty money in her house, she put the both of them out.

Live by the streets, die by the streets. That was my mother's only word to my brothers before they both left our home.

Before my brothers turned twenty-one, Kaleo was addicted to crack and Karreem was doing time for dealing drugs. The night of his arrest, Karreem was driving down Forrest Drive in his hoopty, thinking he was invincible. Weed smoke filled his car while he was pumping some Rare Essence in his speakers. He made a left turn onto Bywater Road and didn't even get past Safeway before the sirens and flashing lights approached him. They stopped him for a blown out tail light. Karreem knew he was fucked because the officers smelled the weed way before getting to his driver side window. That was least of his worries. Karreem had drugs in the trunk at a street value of $25,000. Karreem was no longer a juvenile so he had to do a grown man sentence.

My sister, Vicky and I were four years apart. We looked out for each other and did everything together until she got too old for me being her shadow. In the back of her mind she was too grown for me and wanted to hang out with her friends. She was into boys, hard! She would sneak out of the window just to chill with them. That never changed anything between us. I waited until she got home to be my best friend again. I even helped her hide her pregnancy from our mother when she was a senior at Annapolis High.

Being the youngest child at home, my mother kept me pinned under her thumb. Home, school, and my part-time job at Macy's was where my mother wanted me to be. I couldn't go anywhere else without her permission. I hated that! She tried hard to get me through school without a baby and a drug problem. When I graduated from high school, my mother felt so relieved.

~~~~~~~~

I was working my daily job at Macy's one busy afternoon when I saw two men at the register, buying damn near every pair of Roc A Wear jeans in their size. I was straightening up and folding a pile of khakis on the display table. I caught eye contact with the shorter one, Rick Baker. He was a hustler. He started out with my brothers. They all were really close growing up. I never knew how much he liked himself some Moni when I was younger.

I focused on something else because I knew he was about to come talk to me. I turned around and started refolding all of the shirts on the display table next to the khakis. Just when I thought they were gone, I felt a tap on my shoulder. I slowly put the shirts down and turned around.

"Whassta deal ma?"

He was in my face wearing a black and red-stripped Polo shirt and a pair of khaki pants. He had that sexy thug thing going for him.

"Can I help you?"

I stood there blushing.

3

"You can let me come holla at you sometimes," he said while showed off his sexy smile.

"For what?" Looking him up and down.

"For you. For me." He winked. "Know what I mean?"

No I don't. I don't think Lexie would be cool with that idea." I was referring to his son's mother.

His friend was walking around trying to give his man some time to talk to me but I knew he was being nosey from the grin on his face. Rick reached into his shopping bag and pulled out a smaller shopping bag.

"What if I tell you that I bought this for you?"

"I can't accept gifts from customers. It's against store's policy."

He reached into the bag and pulled out the seven hundred dollar Coach bag that I admired everyday when I walked past the handbags and accessories department. I tried to hide my smile but he saw right through me. He pulled out a business card and handed it to me.

"I hope you use my number," he handing me the bag and headed towards the exit doors.

Chapter One
Moni

It was quarter after six when I left my job. When I walked out of the door, I heard a deep voice calling my name.

"Moni. Yo wait up," Rick called from the passenger seat of a black Escalade with dark tinted windows.

His friend pulled up to the door. When he stopped, the rims were still spinning. I stood there as Rick stepped out of the car. He walked over to me with a smile that made my knees weak. He was about six foot tall, dark brown complexion and he had a body like Ray Lewis. He was nicely built and far from scrawny. I felt like I had been watching him walk from the car for about five minutes. I was in a daze.

"I couldn't leave without talking to you," he moistening his lips with his tongue.

"So you a stalker now?" I asked, acting like he didn't impress me.

"You can call me whatever you want, ok. Just as long as you call me. I don't care when."

I smiled. I looked down at the bag with the Coach bag in it and then I looked at Rick.

"When should I call you?" I questioned with a naughty grin.

I was eager to see what else he had in store for me.

"Tonight," he replied. His smile was enticing.

I didn't know what was wrong with me. I knew I was going to get with Rick soon and I was looking forward to it. I knew it was wrong since he still fucked with his baby momma but it was something about him that made me want to know him a little better. Intimately. Up close and personal. I felt guilty and ashamed of the thoughts I was having about him and his smooth, sexy lips.

There was always something about a fine man who dressed nicely that really turned me on. I controlled my temptations until now but the sunshine in between my thighs was ready to set. I didn't know what was going to happen but I knew one thing, I wanted him something terrible.

~~~~~~~~

The first time Rick snuck into my room, I felt like a woman trying to be grown and sexy, but I really was nothing more than nervous and shy.

It was October 13, 2005. A girl never forgot her first time.

"What you so scared of?"

6

"I don't want to be your next baby mother!" I looked him up and down.

"Girl, I'm not gonna knock you up!"

At that time, he was laughing at me.

"It's not funny! I'm very serious. I'm too young to be a mother."

"Whatever ma. Just admit it. You scared you gon' fall in love with a nigga."

"Yeah, whatever!"

"Then come here," he smiled while pulling me close to him.

Rick unzipped my dress, beginning from the nape of my neck down to the end of my spine. He placed both his hands on my shoulders and carefully slid the sleeves off my shoulders. The dress fell down to my waist then hit the floor. Everything began to move in slow motion after he turned me around to face him. I stood before him with my eyes closed, wearing a purple lace bra and panty set. He unsnapped my bra from the back then pulled my panties down. He carried me over to my twin size bed.

He began softly kissing my pussy and it surprised me how wet I got between my thighs. He made me feel like I was melting in an overheated tropical fantasy. I started moaning softly when he sucked my neck until the marks of passion surfaced. He began kissing my breast and pulling my nipples with his teeth. He fingered me a few times to see if I was ready for him to enter me.

Rick took off his pants and pulled a condom from the back pocket. My body started trembling.

"You okay?"

"I'm scared." I was looking deeply into his eyes.

"Scared of what? I won't hurt you."

"This is my first time."

He looked at me in disbelief at first, and then he thought for a minute.

"Damn, Moni. You want me to stop?"

"No," I quickly stated, not needing a moment to think.

Rick stopped for a moment and ran his hands up and down my body. He admired my caramel complexion, thick thighs, big breasts, and full lips. His touch made me feel really good about taking our friendship to the next level.

Bringing my virginity to his attention seemed to have made him a little more cautious with me. He entered me an inch at a time until all nine inches were hidden deep inside of me. I was in tears from the pleasure I received from the pain. I dug into his back trying to hold on to him.

"Oh my fucking God!" he yelled.

It was a battle trying to control his nut and try to be easy with me. The tightness of my pussy made it hard for him. Eight minutes of his long strokes had him coming fast.

To my mother, I was her good girl. Little did she know, the boy next door was always creeping into my window on the late night. That's what I loved about the lower level houses on the 800 block of Brooke Court. Easy access! Three taps on my window and I would open it for Rick.

~~~~~~~~

Rick and I were a couple and I was almost everywhere he was. He was starting to get wrapped up in me and his son's mom was about to start a war.

One night, I went to a club in Baltimore with my girls KeKey and Stephanie. We were standing in line waiting to get our pictures taken when I heard a girl talking about me.

"That's the bitch right there. She works at the mall."

"I would drop her ass right here," another girl joined in.

I looked over to the girls and the one in the middle didn't say a word. She had on tight fitted jean Capri pants and an orange and white halter-top. She had on a pair of heels that matched the orange in her shirt. She was small and petite. She had an evil look on her face. At first I didn't recognize her because she wasn't looking like her usual hood rat self. It was my first time being that close to Lexie. I'd only seen her from a distance. I didn't sweat her attitude. I went back to laughing with my girls and then I heard them talking again.

"I'on't know what the fuck Rick see in that fat bitch."

I looked in their direction because I couldn't believe they were talking about me. I was far from fat. I was thick in all the right places.

I had more curves than all the girls in Lexie's crew. I called their hating straight jealousy.

My girl Stephanie heard her and asked, "Is there a problem?"

"Tell that bitch to leave other people men alone then we wouldn't have a problem." She rolled her eyes and put her hand on her hip.

"Tell that bitch she can speak for herself." KeKey, my very outspoken friend screamed on her. "It ain't my girl's fault ya girl don't know how to keep her man."

"You better watch who the fuck you talking to," Lexie's friend stated bluntly. She was pissed off.

"Look! We don't need to cause a scene." I insisted while try to calm everyone down.

Lexie surprised me when she finally spoke. "I know you didn't think you were gon' get away with fuckin' with my man, bitch!" She got in my face.

Her friends got loud and my friends got louder. Before I knew it, security rushed through the crowd and started pushing us towards the door. We got kicked out. Steph wanted to wait for Lexie but I told her I didn't want any drama with the bitch. We decided to go out to eat. When we arrived at TGIF, I stepped out of KeKey's blue Honda Civic. We were walking towards the entrance until we heard the sound of car doors slamming shut.

"Where's all that mouth ya'll bitches had in the club?" Lexie's friend yelled.

Before I could turn around, Lexie and one of her friends jumped on me. I fell to the ground and my head hit the black top. I felt dizzy but something made me get up. I had never been in a fight before except for with my sister when I was younger. I didn't know I had the strength but I pushed them off of me. When I stood up, Lexie punched me in my mouth. I was so furious that I punched her so hard she felt to the ground. Her friend tried to help her up and I kicked her in her leg and made her fall to the ground, too. Steph went to KeKey's car and pulled out her baseball bat and started swinging. Lexie and her friends limped back to the car and sped off.

I looked at my reflection in the window of a white Cadillac that was in the parking lot. My left cheek was swollen and my lip was busted. My already round face looked like the size of a four hundred pound person. I looked at Steph and she looked like she handled her business because the only thing they did to her was rip her shirt a little. She was showing her lilac laced bra. KeKey had scratches on her arms and her face.

We got ourselves together just in time. Right when we were turning out of the parking lot, two police cars pulled up in front of the restaurant. My heart was racing. I was hoping no one saw what car we got in.

Chapter Two
Moni

I was sitting at the light about to turn onto Jennifer Road. I was leaving Westfield Shopping Mall when I damn near hit the car in front of me. I was startled when I heard the loud screams.

"Get the fuck out of the car!"

I slammed on the breaks and looked to the right of me.

Oh shit! I thought.

It was Lexie and she pulled up right next to me. Why of all days did she chose to beef with me while I was by myself? I looked into her car and saw four bitches mean mugging me.

"Get the fuck out of the car, bitch!"

At this point we were holding up traffic. Then, all of a sudden, Lexie's go hard best friend Te Te jumped out of the car and started kicking my car real hard. I heard the dents. The sound of her foot against my car was more like a brick.

I reached for my cell and called KeKey.

"KeKey! I'm outside of the mall and these bitches ready to get in my shit."

"Bitch! I told you not to fuck with them bitches," she yelled into the phone.

"Bitch! Just get the fuck out here. Call the crew 'cause a bitch ready get fucked up!" I yelled.

"We on our way!" KeKey sounded like a solider for life.

I was panicking like shit! I didn't want to look scared so I opened my car door and started popping mad shit!

"Ya'll bitches can't fuck with me! Don't be mad 'cause I got ya man!" I yelled, giving them so much attitude.

Before I knew it, Steph came walking towards our cars, squeezing past the crowd we had drawn to our drama.

"Is there a fucking problem?" She yelled while holding up her box cutter.

"What the fuck you gone do with that?" Te Te asked, already knowing what the deal was.

"Step if you want and you'll surely find out!"

I didn't know where Steph came from but she was my lifesaver. We broke out before Jake, the police, made their presence on the scene. I'd never been so happy to hear police sirens. They broke up our drama for the night but that definitely wasn't the end of the beef.

~~~~~~~~

"Moni! I know you ain't gone let no little bitches put fear in you heart!"

Rick was looking at me like he was trying to figure me out.

"I'm not. I'm just tryna chill for a minute. Ya baby mom be on some other shit!"

"Boo, fuck her! You know this shit is all about you," He smiled, flashing the cash he had in his pocket.

I must admit, the money was the attraction to him. I saw dollar signs like crazy. Rick was always flashing money and he was always spending it on me. Money was a good look for gold diggers and stick up kids. I never considered myself a gold digger but I didn't know why I loved Rick's money so much.

"Come on, get in." Rick motioned with his head to get into his Escalade.

"No!"

"Girl, get in so I can take ya ass shopping."

I started blushing and covered my face.

"Where we going?"

"Yeah, I knew that shit would change your mind."

He unlocked his door while I climbed in like a kid on the way to the ice cream shop.

"It didn't change my mind. I just wanted to spend some time with you," I was popping my bubble gum. I leaned over the seat and kissed Rick on his neck.

"Don't get shit started, ma."

"I'm not, daddy." I blew into his ear.

"Stop fucking around!"

I loved doing shit to make him horny.

I sat back in the seat as T.I. filled the Escalade from the CD player. I reclined my seat to get comfy. It was going to be a long ride from Annapolis to New York. We took that trip often. I was always shopping in New York so the bitches in Annapolis wouldn't rock the same shit I rocked. Rick went to New York to cop some coke from his connect.

I was never allowed near their meetings. Rick would put me in a hotel room. He'd come back to the room to rest his head. The next morning, we were on the road before the sun came up. Never did the coke come back with us. Rick would pay Rita, a crack fiend, $500 plus train tickets both ways. She carried the coke in her pussy. She was loyal to Rick and his connect.

Chapter Three
Moni

It was almost six p.m. when I decided to get out of the indoor pool at the Wingate by Wyndham at LaGuardia Airport in Flushing, NY. I dried off with the fresh white towel and put my bathrobe around my body. Just as I was tying the robe around my waist, I felt strong arms wrap around me. It startled me at first until he whispered in my ear.

"Damn you so beautiful!"

I turned to Rick and he kissed me gently.

"What are you doing back so early?"

"I wanted to take you out before we head home in the morning."

"Really?" I was anxious.

"Yeah, we never do anything after we come from shopping and handling some business so let's do some'in different." He hugged me tighter.

We hurried up to the room so we could shower and change into something nice. When I unlocked the door, I turned the lights on and

16

noticed a long white box with a big red bow on it. I gave Rick a love tap on his shoulder.

"What did you get me?" I was so blissful.

"I got you a lil' some'in while I was out. Open it up!"

He sat on the edge of the bed while he watched me with anticipation. I untied the bow and set it aside. I carefully removed the lid to the box.

"Hurry up, girl!"

"Don't rush me, nigga!"

I pulled the tissue paper out of the box and revealed a long white spaghetti strap dress with a pair of two-carat, princess cut diamond earrings. I jumped up and down with excitement.

"Awe, Rick! Thank you baby."

"That's not it. Look under the bed."

I bent down and pulled up the bed skirt. It was a shoebox. I pulled it out and opened it. There were size eight, five-inch heel, white Prada shoes.

"Ooh, baby!" I hugged him. "These the ones from the magazine!" I yelled. "How did you remember?"

"I just did. Now come here and thank me properly."

Rick pulled me to him and started tugging at the belt around my robe. Once he got it open, he slid it off my shoulders and then it fell to the floor. I was wearing a yellow bikini bathing suit that snapped in between my breast. He unsnapped it so fast like he had years of practice. I crossed my arms behind his head as he kissed my breast and nibbled on my nipples.

Rick picked me up and sat me on his shoulders. He put my legs around his face while he licked my clit. I palmed his head for balance. He squeezed my round ass while twirling his tongue over my erect clit. He stroked his stiff tongue in my pussy harder and faster. He licked and sucked me until he made me come on his tongue and face. My body trembled on his shoulders. He dropped me on the bed and climbed on top of me.

"Turn that ass ova," he whispered.

Rick spread my legs to both sides of the bed. He finger fucked me as he licked me from the back to the front. He made my toes curl and had me griping the sheets.

"Oh my God!" I yelled. "Don't stop!"

Chills covered my body when he started darting his stiff tongue in and out of my pussy. He didn't stop until I came again.

"Oh my God! What are you doing to me?"

Rick got behind me and filled me up with his hardness. Each inch, we became closer until he was so deep that I thought he would come through my stomach. His slow rhythm turned fast and then faster. His strokes got so powerful, the headboard sounded as if it was going to go through the wall into the next room.

"Uuugggghhhh!" Rick yelled as he came and squirted all over my ass.

We collapsed next to one another.

Chapter Four
Rick

I watched Moni sleep for about thirty minutes before I crept out the door to our hotel room. She looked so peaceful sleeping. I hated leaving her alone but a nigga had business to attend to. Once I closed the door, I pulled my cell from my pocket to make a quick call.

"Damn, nigga! What took you so long?" she wined.

"What I tell you 'bout questioning me?"

"You said you would be a quick minute, nigga! That was like three damn hours ago!"

"Look, bitch, I'm tired of going through this shit with you. Meet me in front of the telly and hurry ya ass up!" I demanded.

KeKey really knew how to stress a nigga out. She threw fits like she was five years old. Every time we made the trip to New York, she had her hands and her lip poked out. Who knew a night of some good head would turn into a constant headache. I should have just beat the dick and kept it moving.

At first, KeKey was like a little ride or die chick but then she turned needy. KeKey was from around the way. She used to help me bag my shit and hook me up with coke connect from out of town. As close as her and Moni were, she never found out about KeKey fucking me. We were so close that she thought she was more like my little sista than anything. She trusted us to be alone together.

One night about six months back, KeKey stayed over my house with Moni because her mother was tripping on her hard for going to the club. They got in a big fight out in the street by the rec center. After her mom gave her a serious beat down, she came crying to Moni and me. I gave them some dough to hang out for the night so I could have some time to handle business.

When I got home, Moni was already knocked out. KeKey was stretched on my couch with one of my white tees on. Her chocolate round ass was showing threw her black boy shorts. Her hair was a little wild but it still got my dick rock hard.

I sat near her feet and she jumped when she felt me. She pulled the blanket over her exposed body. She shyly covered up and lay back down.

"You and ya mom cool now?"

"No!" She rolled her eyes. "She told me I'm nothing but a fast tramp because she found out I was fucking with this nigga, when I should have been at the Moni's house."

"Fucking? Girl who you fucking?"

"Buck. We hooked up after the club," she was proud.

"Buck? That soft ass nigga? You fucking him?"

"Yeah. Why?"

"That nigga is mad soft, boo. He ain't shit but a look out kid."

"Oh yeah?" She laughed. "He told me you had him on the count."

"Yeah right! That nigga can't even weigh the blow so why the fuck you think he doing some grow men shit?"

I went in the kitchen and got us both of MGD from the refrigerator. When I joined KeKey on the couch, she was at the coffee table rolling a blunt. I didn't know she smoked but she took two blunts to the head. We both were high off the weed and my dick wanted to feel that pussy.

KeKey was shy at first but she broke out of her shell when I used a little force to make her lie back on the couch. I spread her long chocolate legs and pulled her boy shorts off. Once I exposed her already dripping pussy, I stuck two fingers in. I knew she was fucking with some little dick because her walls were tight around my fingers. Her moans slipped out of her full lips.

"Oh my God, Rick!" she whispered. "We gonna get caught if Moni wakes up."

"No we won't, shawty. She out for the count."

I took my shirt off her body and smiled at her bare nipples. They were hard and waiting for me to tease them. I sucked her so hard she begged me for more pleasure.

"Don't stop, Rick! It feels so good!"

"Oh yeah? You wanna feel this dick?"

"Yes..."

On the floor, I put her legs in the air and spread them like wings. Once I put dick in her, she was shacking and moaning like crazy. I put my t-shirt over her mouth to shut her up. Her moans were then muffled. I gave her long, deep dick strokes until she bust and fell asleep on the floor.

After covering her up, I went into the bathroom and washed the scent of KeKey's sweet pussy off in the shower. I dried off and then went to my room to find Moni still sleeping. She was curled up looking so beautiful with her hair tied up and her arms wrapped around my pillow. I got in the bed with her and fell asleep with her in my arms.

~~~~~~~~

"What took ya ass so long?"

KeKey had me sitting in the cut waiting for her too damn long. When I jumped in the ride, she rolled her eyes at me and pulled off.

"Was I complaining when you spent all that damn money on Moni and ain't get me shit?"

"What the fuck! Why everything gotta be about you?"

"Because I'm ya girl just as much as she is."

I knew she lost her fucking mind.

"Don't keep running ya mouth!" I insisted. "You gon' fine ya shit real fucked up."

"Whatever nigga! You keep singing that same shit."

She put her hand to my face and before I realized it, I punched her in the mouth. Everything paused. KeKey had slammed on the brakes, making us both jerk forward.

"Bitch!" she yelled while swinging on me.

I felt bad for putting my hands on her but she changed that quickly.

"I know you didn't just put ya hands on me! After all the shit I did for you."

I tried to hug her to calm her down but she kept swinging and zapping out on me. We sat in the car in silence. KeKey kept staring at me like she wanted to kill me. I should have felt bad when she started crying but I didn't. I pulled over on 495 Long Island Expressway. I got out the car and then walked around the driver side to open her door. I pulled her to her feet and hugged her.

"Boo, you know I didn't mean it. I'm sorry," I forced myself to say.

She leaned her head on my shoulder and didn't say anything else. I stepped back from her and then I reached into my back pocket and pulled out a little blue box with a white gold necklace with a three caret canary yellow princess cut diamond. Her eyes light up from the sparkles.

"Oh my God! Rick, this is so fucking cute!"

"See, you thinking I didn't get you shit."

"I know. You really do be thinking about me." She smiled.

"I don't bring you on these trips for nothing, shawty."

The truth was, KeKey's uncle, Max had some serious connect with some niggas in Baltimore, D.C., Philly and New York. She handled business like one of those Lil' Kim types of chicks. All those out of town niggas wanted a taste of KeKey. She was about 5'7 with skin the color of dark chocolate. Her frame was thick. Her hips were wide, her waist was thin, ass and tits were both fat. She had that ghetto girl attitude but when it came to business, she was on point. She got that from her uncle.

Chapter Five
Rick

It didn't take KeKey and I long before we pulled up in the Flushing Meadow Corona Park. This was one of the regular spots were I got up with Sal. Sal was a middle aged, fat dude who was balding more and more each time I saw him. His shiny head had a few strands of hair on the side. He combed that back in a ponytail.

Sal never got out of his 2007 black Lincoln Town car with illegally dark tents and we never talked directly to each other. KeKey got out of the car with a briefcase full of Franklin faces. Tony, Sal's right hand man, got out the car with a briefcase. I watched them sit their briefcases down and then hugged each other. Tony whispered something in her ear and she smiled. She playfully hit him in his arm and then they shared a good-bye hug. Tony picked up KeKey's briefcase and walked back to the car. KeKey returned to the car with the briefcase full of coke.

Sal's car pulled off before KeKey could open the door to our car. When she got in, I kissed her soft check.

"Good looking out shawty."

"Ain't nothing boo. You know I got you." She smiled.

We stopped by a near by gas station so KeKey could drop me off. I trusted shawty to get the drugs back to Maryland so I caught a cab back to the hotel where Moni was waiting for me. KeKey called me before the cab dropped me off to tell me she met up with Rita. Rita got on the next train out of town.

KeKey went back to the car rental spot and gave the car back. She had her car in a near by garage. She took that drive back to MD. I was proud of how much she grew in the business. I never had to tell her what I wanted done. She handled business like she could read my mind.

I was sticking the key in our room door when my cell stared vibrating.

"Yo," I answered.

"What up nigga?" It was my right hand nigga, Ace.

"Yo that shit's right." He played it cool.

"Good nigga. I'm glad to hear that!" We hung up.

It was our way of letting me know every transaction was running smoothly. I didn't play that sloppy business shit. That's how niggas got set the fuck up. I got eyes on everybody working for me. I trusted nobody.

When I walked in our room, Moni was putting on her new dress. She looked surprised to see me back so early from handling business. I smiled when I saw her. She was one of the few people I didn't know what I would do without.

"Hey baby, you done doing you?" She came over to kiss me.

"Yeah princess. It didn't take long at all." I told her and then kissed her cheek.

"Cool. I'm glad you back before our dinner reservations."

"Where you make reservations at?"

"Stella D'Argento Restaurant."

"Oh yeah, I had a taste for some Italian." I tapped her ass.

"You know this my favorite Italian spot." She was excited.

She leaned in to hug me and I kissed the tip of her nose. I enjoyed watching Moni getting fresh for our date. She was doing it up with all new shit on, courtesy of my money. I didn't want Moni shitting on me so I stepped my style up for the evening. I had on black with tan pin stripe Stacy Adam suit that was tailor made and a pair of Stacy Adams black Milo shoes. I put on a small platinum chain to accent the suit.

Moni was excited to be on my arm for the evening. We arrived at the restaurant about ten minutes before our reservations. The atmosphere was nice, definitely romantic with candlelight at the table. I ordered an expensive bottle of red wine. Moni sipped her one glass the whole time while I finished the bottle. I didn't even get a buzz. Moni ordered the Veal Stella D'Argento and I had the Osso Bucco.

After we left the spot, we drove to the Queens Museum of Arts. I thought Moni was out of her mind when she told me that's where we were going next. She was excited about the exhibits because she studied some pieces in college.

Just when the evening was feeling good, my cell kept vibrating. I silenced the called three times when I saw KeKey's name pop up on my screen. I excused myself to take the call when she called again for the forth time.

"What's up?" I answered.

"It's about time you answered!" She was in a pissed mood.

"Yeah? Why, what's going on?" I questioned.

"I wanted to let you know Rita's home already. She brought me the...."

I gave her ass the dial tone. I was pissed off she tried pull some shit like that. I planned to get a new cell when I get home and KeKey wasn't gon' have the number.

When I got up with Moni, she was pricing some art. She thought money came easy. I quickly reminded her it didn't.

"What you doing?" I startled her.

"I'm asking about this piece right here. Won't this be cute in your house?"

"Where the hell it's gon' go at?"

"I wasn't trying to buy it, I just was curious of the price."

"Yeah fucking right, shawty spend a lot."

On our way back to the hotel, Moni's cell kept ringing. I looked her up and down like I knew she better handle her phone. My first instincts were it was some nigga trying get at her. Then she was getting pissed off because every time she answered, the person on the other end would hang up.

"Who the fuck is this!" she yelled into her phone.

They hung up again. I took the cell from her and checked it out. They called from a blocked number so the screen showed line one ringing. I thought it was KeKey trying to pay me back from the punch I threw at her. When it rung again, I answered.

"Yo, who this?"

Dial tone.

"It's probably your stank ass baby's mother sitting home with nothing better to do." She rolled her eyes and folded her arms. "That bitch always hating on me!"

"I'll handle it princess. Chill out."

"I will baby."

Moni stopped thinking about the calls but I wanted to know what was up. I was always thinking somebody out to get me. If they couldn't get at me, they would try get at my princess. I couldn't let shit happen to her.

Before we got back to the telly, we picked up some cheesecake. Moni couldn't wait to get in our room so she could put a fork in it. She stuffed her mouth with her cheesecake, some of mine and then passed out. I couldn't sleep. Business was on my mind.

I did a lot of people dirty so I always slept with one eye open. I watched Moni sleep for a couple hours before I dozed off. I was anxiously waiting our return to Maryland. New York wasn't feeling like home.

Chapter Six
Moni

I was sitting in the back of my Psychology class when I overheard a couple of fellas talking about me. I thought it was cute to be someone's crush. Jay was the average height, light skinned one with a close cut fade. He had waves in his hair and was very sexy. His dimples made him even sexier.

"Moni looking right in them Apple Bottom jeans," Jay tried to whisper.

"Moni always looking right, homie!" his friend co-signed.

"True that but she making me wanna get with her in those jeans."

"Nigga, you must wanna get ya head busted!" His friend laughed. "That's Rick's girl and he don't play that shit!"

"Who the fuck is Rick?"

"That nigga from Naptown. You know Rick!"

"Oh yeah. He don't put no fear in my heart. He breathes the same air I do."

I thought the conversation was funny. I thought Jay was brave for not worrying about my relationship with Rick. Whenever somebody heard I was Rick's girl, they either respected me right away or hated me right away.

When I thought the conversation was over, I started reading my textbook. I started flipping the page and knocked my pencil in the floor. All eyes turned on me and then Jay rushed to my desk to pick up my pencil.

"Here you go, beautiful." He smiled.

"Thank you." I blushed.

My body turned hot as lust covered it. I shook the thoughts until he kissed my hand. I felt an instant wetness that I was almost embarrassed of.

"Anything for you and I do mean anything." He gave me a sexy smile.

Jay went back to his seat as people continued watching like we were on a soap opera. I continued reading from the text and then I noticed the small piece of paper folded into two halves. I acted as if the phone number he wrote on the paper didn't matter but inside I was blushing like a little girl.

~~~~~~~~

I was shutting the door to Rick's ride when he started.

"Who the fuck is this nigga giving you his number in class?" he yelled. "Is this what my money paying for? You getting nigga's numbers and shit?"

He was jealous.

"Hello to you too Rick." I hated how he kept eyes on me all the time.

"Fuck that, Moni, don't play me!" He snatched my bag from in between my feet.

"I know I better not find his number in this bag." He stared at me hard.

"I didn't keep the number Rick. He was just being nice," I insisted.

"Fuck being nice. Everybody knows what's up with us."

When he didn't find the number he searched my cell phone and I was pissed off because he was treating me like a little kid.

"Baby, I told you I didn't keep the number." I leaned over and gave him a kiss on his cheek.

"Al-ight shawty." He took a deep breath. "I believe you." He was lying.

"Good baby. You know I'm ya girl."

"Yeah, well tomorrow you're changing classes."

"Okay." I didn't know what else to say.

The more money Rick made, the less trusting he became of the people surrounding him. I considered myself lucky he still let me go to college. He made me stop working at the mall about two months back because he said too many niggas was in my face. At first I thought it was cute to have people watching out for me. Rick always told me somebody might be out to get me since I was his chick but eventually, the

33

protection turned into babysitting. I couldn't scratch my ass without Rick knowing about it.

I was mad at Rick for being so controlling with me. He knew it but I wouldn't speak on it. I was his princess. I was the closest person to him so I didn't want him to feel that lack of security with me.

We were sitting in his house eating some Chinese take out when he pulled out a knot of money with a rubber band holding it together.

"Here, baby. I want you buy something nice for you and get your hair done."

"All this for me?" My mouth dropped.

It had to be at least ten thousand of spending money. That was the most money he gave me to blow on myself. I guess he was feeling guilty about making me stop working and his attitude lately. I quickly forgot why I was mad at him.

Rick used to give me spending money here and there but it was like a few hundred or at the most a thousand. I used to blow it all in two days but little Miss Princess got wiser. Now, I send some money to my sister, my mom, and to my bank account. Thanks to Rick, I had at least twenty thousand in savings.

"Damn baby! Business must be nice."

"Fuck nice! Business is the shit right now!"

"I know that's right baby!"

After we finished eating, I got up to put my money in my new baby blue, navy blue, tan, and white Coach bag. Rick was in the room with the door closed handling business I guess. I tapped on the door to let him know I was heading out.

I drove to my cousin's Londa shop and got her hook my hair up in a fresh roller wrap set. My girl was gifted when it came to some hair. She kept her best styles for me. The little chicken heads from around the way would be so jealous of the hook up she gave me.

"You really out did yourself, my favorite cousin." I admired her work in the mirror of her hair station.

"You know I can't have my little cousin out here looking a hot mess!"

She laughed while wiping the hair off of me.

On my way out the door, I paid for my hairstyle and tipped my cousin with a fifty. She gave me a hug.

"See you next weekend." She waved to me as I left out.

Damn I was looking like a little sexy mami. I checked myself out in my car window. I had on a baby blue sweater, dark blue jeans made by Baby Phat, and a new pair of almond UGG Tess boots. I could see why Rick kept a close eye on me. My butter soft skin and all this thickness, I was a ghetto fabulous diva. I was on my way to the bank when my cell kept ringing.

"Hello."

There was no answer. That shit was getting old fast. The next two calls were from a blocked number so I didn't answer. *Rick's childish ass baby mother.* I thought. I wish that trick would grow up and stop hating on me.

After depositing money into my sister's account and my mother's account, I had five g's left to put in mine. On my way out of the bank, my cell rung again. This time I recognized the caller.

"What's up KeKey?"

"Hey bitch!" she sung into my ear. "Where the fuck you at?"

"Handling business bitch!"

"I'm hungry. Meet me at Nordstrom's. That salmon salad we had last week was the shit."

"Yeah that was good. Plus, I want look at some shoes when we finished eating," I told her.

"There you go spending ya man's dough again."

She was hating and I was laughing to myself.

"My man got a lot to go around. He broke me off properly before I left his house."

"I know that's right bitch! So hit my phone when you in the parking garage."

"Alright girl." We hung up.

Chapter Seven
Moni

I had just hung up my cell with KeKey to let her know I was parking my car. I found a spot about two rows over from hers. When I stepped out, I chirped the alarm button. I glanced in my car window to check myself out before entering the store.

I thought I was seeing a ghost when a reflection appeared behind me. Then I damn near shit myself when I heard his gun cock.

"I see you, bitch, thinking you shitting on a nigga, right?" the deep voice said. I didn't respond. He pushed the gun deeper to the back of my head. "I know you heard me, bitch. Gimme all ya shit!" he yelled. I handed him my purse as tears poured down my face. "You think a nigga s'pose to have sympathy for you? I don't. I don't give a fuck about you Moni."

Damn, the bastard knew my name. That made me curious about the stick up kid. "Turn around bitch," he spat.

I turned to see Jay-R in a black stocking covering his face. I couldn't believe he thought I wouldn't recognize him. Jay-R used to be a little nigga that ran for Rick. Rick didn't trust him so he always had him doing grimy shit.

"Tell that bitch nigga I said he ain't shit but a bitch nigga!" Referring to Rick.

He swung at me to punch me in the face but I felt to ground before he could hit me. Jay-R and his little stick up friend ran when they heard the sirens from the mall's security trucks.

I was on the ground crying when I heard a familiar voice. "Moni! What happened?"

"I got robbed." I continued crying.

"I was wondering what the fuck was taking you so long." She helped me up and hugged me. "Don't cry, Moni. We'll get those niggas."

KeKey went into her purse and she got her cell phone for me. I called Rick and told him what happened.

"Damn baby. Get KeKey to bring you over my spot."

He was worried.

"The security guard said I have to wait for the police."

"Fuck the police. We'll handle those niggas our way."

"Okay." I cried out.

I was more pissed off more than scared. That little bitch had the keys to my car, my purse, and four hundred in cash. I was happy I dropped money off at the bank before going to the mall. I kept having flashbacks of the robbery. In KeKey's car, I was leaned against the window crying. My body was so hot like I was running a fever. It felt like steam was lifting off me.

~~~~~~~~

When we got up with Rick, he was getting off the phone with Ace. They were making plans to put a hit on Jay-R. I couldn't recall ever being happy about violence but when I thought about what those bastards did to me, I was overjoyed. We rode with Rick to a vacant building close to downtown. We got out of the car and looked around.

"Baby, this is creepy," I told Rick.

"It's cold in this stank ass place," KeKey complained. "Where Ace at anyway?"

Rick didn't respond to either of us. He remained quiet like he always does when those wheels started turning in his mind.

It didn't take long before Ace rolled up in this big, ugly red truck looking like he got it from Fred Sanford. I wondered where he found that old dude with the truck. He must have gotten it from a crack head for exchange for a hit. Ace stepped out of the passenger side, pulled his fitted cap down on his eyebrows and then walked to the back of the truck. Ace was serious when it came to beating ass. Most niggas feared him just by from his build. Ace was about 6'4. His skin was the color of dark chocolate and he was about three hundred or more pounds. His hands were the size of a baseball glove. You could imagine when those things were balled into a fist, they could cause some serious damage.

Ace pulled the two men from the back of the truck so hard they felt to the ground. Rick,

KeKey, and I stood there watching the beating Ace delivered until I heard his gun cock. My whole body covered with fear. I leaned into Rick's arms to cover my eyes. I still heard the click and then the loud bang. I smelled the gun fire and then he did it again. I heard the click and then the loud bang a second time and both men were silent. My emotions were shattered. It was the first time I witnessed death and I didn't want to see it again.

I looked at Jay-R while he bled from his mouth and his gun shot wound in his temple. I wondered why Jay-R wanted to rob me. He had to know Rick would retaliate. It was like he wrote his death sentence. Everybody knew Rick didn't play when it came to his princess and his family.

Ace stood their staring at the bodies like he wanted to be sure they were breathless. He scared me with the evil in his eye. He looked like he was wishing Jay-R and his homeboy a life in hell. KeKey walked over to him and put her hand on his shoulder gently to make him aware of her presence.

"We gotta be out, killa nigga," she called him jokingly.

She stepped over their bodies like it was nothing. She acted as if it wasn't a first for her. I was still in shock but she was nonchalant.

Rick went to his ride and got a bag out. He walked over towards KeKey and Ace.

"Get the shells up KeKey." He gave her the bag to put them in.

She looked around for shell casing and when she spotted one, she went to pick it up with her hand.

"Fuck!" she screamed. "These shells hot nigga!"

Ace and Rick laughed at her. She rolled her eyes.

"Ya'll can be some bitches sometimes," she proclaimed.

KeKey went to the crack head's truck to find a pair of work gloves.

"Perfect," She spook loudly.

Once she got the gloves on her hands, she continued searching for shells and picking them up. She turned into someone I didn't know. She was too excited about helping clean up the crime. KeKey was acting as if she just did something that would award her with high merits.

Jay-R made a bad choice and it cost him his life. Out of fear, Rick was the first person I thought should know about the robbery. I felt guilty for not letting the police handle their business. I was just as much responsible for the death of those young black men.

Everything seemed like a video game. Everybody was happy about putting some young black men to rest way before their time. Rick treated Ace and KeKey like it was a job well done when he peeled off some dollars for their pocket. I couldn't believe he gave KeKey that kind of money. She was smiling like she hit the lottery. As for Jay-R and his friend, game over.

Chapter Eight
Rick

I knew that little nigga Jay-R was trying send a message to me. He was hostile about me getting with his baby momma, Quana, about a month ago. I couldn't believe he had the audacity to get me back by robbing my princess. If that small time nigga could get at her, I could imagine who was plotting on causing Moni some harm.

This shit was all my fault. I should have just kept it moving but I had to get shawty's number. I was chilling in VIP with the crew up in H2O when I saw lil' momma doing her thing on the dance floor in front of the VIP section. Quana had a fat ass, titties, and legs. She had a face like an angel and a body like a stripper. She rolled and bounced her body to the rhythm of the latest club banger. She worked her body like she was getting paid for the video. After the song ended, I slipped the bouncer fifty to let her in the VIP section.

Quana left her girls on the dance floor with jealous stares. She sat on my lap and did a little sexy chair dance for me.

"You like that, daddy?" She kept grinding on my dick.

I didn't respond. I let my fingers caress her body until she started moaning.

"That bitch ready bust off from that shit!" Ace yelled to me. "Handle that shit, nigga!"

Quana rubbed her hands over my hard dick in my pants. "You ain't ready for that baby girl," I teased.

"Shit, nigga, I ain't scared of dick."

She never lied! She unzipped my pants and released my dick. She leaned over and deep throated the dick like she was sucking for dollars. She put it down something serious. I was twitching and moaning. She didn't let my dick go until after I released a mouth full of nut. She swallowed it and smiled like she did a job well done. That bitch was nice. I got her number for future dick sucking purposes.

"You gon' call me?" She smiled.

"Fucking right!"

"Don't play nigga."

"I don't play baby girl. How about we get out of here and go to the hotel up the street."

"I can't. My boyfriend supposed to be meeting me up here."

"So what? How he gon' find you in the club with all these ma fuckas in here?"

She giggled while twisting her long braid around her finger. It didn't take much convincing her to leave with me. While in my ride, she played with all the switches and volume for the radio. She acted really immature but those thoughts went out the window when I thought back to the head game she had.

"You're ride is the bomb!" She said while admiring my ride.

"Thanks shawty."

"I hope word don't get back to ya girl that you kicking with me tonight." She rubbed her hand on my leg.

"Word won't and she won't believe it anyway."

"That's what's up! My boyfriend would be mad."

"I ain't thinking 'bout that nigga."

"Me either," she lied.

"Yeah? Okay."

"Seriously," she popped slick.

I left it at that. The hotel was less than ten minutes away. I parked my car and got a room. Quana was right next to me smiling like she was proud to be by my side.

Inside the room it was on. She gave me a lap dance but this time, she took her clothes off. I threw some dollars at her to get her excited. The bouncing her ass had me hypnotized. That ass was firm and round. I wanted to bite it. I pulled her to the bed and turned her on her stomach. She giggled nervously. I rubbed her ass while she moaned softly. I nibbled on her ass and then I slide my tongue up and down the crack of her ass. Her moans grew louder. I stopped when she shivered, came and collapsed.

I shook her by her head to wake that ass up. Wasn't no going to sleep. She pouted for a little but she immediately got into sucking me off. She handled business like she wanted me to come back for more. We spent the next two hours sucking and fucking.

"Damn, I didn't realize what time it was." She panicked.

"Oh yeah, time slipped away when you wildin' out."

"I forgot Jay-R was meeting me at the club."

"That nigga be al-ight."

Quana went into the bathroom to freshen up. When she came out dressed, I went into the bathroom to wash my face, dick, and hands.

We walked out of the hotel and spotted the little nigga Jay-R standing there with his friend looking all heated like a pit bull. He was blowing hot air. I laughed at him.

"Jay-R!" Quana was startled. "What you doing here?"

"Bitch, don't play dumb!" he yelled while pulling her by the arm.

"Get from out front my car before I run that ass over, little nigga." I told him.

"I ain't scared of your little bitch ass." He let me know.

"You need to be," I threatened. "But that's cool. You trained ya bitch well. She suck and fuck like a champ!"

The little nigga jumped at me and Quana stood in between us.

"Get the fuck out my way Q," he screamed.

"Baby, calm down," she pleaded. "It wasn't what you think baby."

Jay-R stepped back. He eyed both of us. Looking us up and down. I was waiting for his little ass to pop slick but he didn't. He looked at his girl once more and hauled off and smacked her in the face. The impact was so loud it sound like it hurt. Quana grabbed her face and started crying.

"I can't believe you put your fucking hands on me!" she yelled. She started swinging her fist trying to land one on his face. He begged and pleaded with her to stop.

"I'm sorry baby," he yelled. Jay-R hugged her and she didn't stop swinging and crying. He looked like a weak ass trying to calm her cry.

"I can't believe you put your fucking hands on me," Her cry turned to a whimper. "I fucking hate you!"

Quana finally stop crying when Jay-R pulled her into his arm, kissed her, and then apologized. That shit was straight out of a movie. I didn't care about either one of them so I was out with the quickness.

It was bitches like Quana that made me not trust them. They lie and scheme worse than a nigga. They smile in each other's face and then they share the same dick, secretly. Bitches claim to be faithful but will fuck one of her man's friends if he ain't swinging dick right. That's why I didn't trust no scandalous ass bitch.

Chapter Nine
KeKey

Sometimes Moni made me sick with her love-is-blind ass. Rick fucked around right in front her face but she just didn't see it. Let a nigga try holla at Moni, Rick would know in two seconds. With a nigga like Rick, Moni needed to keep her eyes open.

Every since I started fucking with Rick, I watched everything he did. I knew his every move. I knew who he was with. I even knew who he was fucking. I guess I was the female version of Rick because I trusted no niggas. Most niggas were whores and they would trade you in when their dick got tired of your pussy. But Rick, he confused me at times. I didn't get the connection with him and Moni because she was all prissy and uppity. She almost seemed like she wasn't raised in the same hood I was raised in. Her family was poor just like mine. But now, she got more name brand shit than a little bit. She gotta have a flashy car, new hair style every week, and different designer purse everyday.

Rick was straight up hood and there was no changing that. He came from dirty money and everything about him screamed, *'get money!'* If it wasn't about money, he didn't want nothing to do with it. I saw that he loved Moni but I didn't know why. He had his share of hood rats and skanky tricks. He switched up chicks like drawers. I guess Rick made sure to have an upgraded version of his baby momma, which was Moni.

Speaking of Rick's baby momma, she was 100% hood rat. Never worked a day for a dollar. She saw dollar signs and she wanted him. Rick was dumb when it came to her. She set that nigga up with a few condoms full of holes in them. She knew she would be set for life being his baby momma. When she started showing in her pregnancy, she moved to Shady Side so no one would know what was up. When the baby was a month old, she moved back to Annapolis and sprung the news on Rick. The baby was a spitting image of Rick but he still got a blood test. No one could knock him for that because his baby momma got around from hood to hood.

~~~~~~~~

An hour earlier I got a call from my uncle Max. He wanted me to handle some business for him with some niggas from Philly. It was my pleasure when I pulled up next to a low rider

48

black 1948 Chevy Fleetline. When the driver told the back seat passenger that it was me next to them, he opened the door and got out the car. The interior was butter leather and camel skin.

I had to make myself stop drooling over the half Black, half Latino cutie. His name was Trent and he stood about 5'10. His shoulders were broad and his arms were bigger than both my legs put together. His built body fascinated me. His skin was smooth and light. His hair was cut into a fade with waves and side burns. He looked good in his tailor made suit and jewelry blinging everywhere. *Good looking out, Uncle Max, for sending me on this mission.*

I stepped out my car with a black mini dress that was cut low almost to my mid stomach. It showed off a whole lot of titty. I had thigh high boots on which gave me an extra four inches in height. When I got close to Trent, he reached for my hand and kissed it.

"I'm gonna enjoy do business with you baby girl." He flirted while flashing his sexy smile.

"I hope so." I giggled and then batted my long lashes at him.

I clicked the lock button and sound the alarm to my car on my key chain. Trent escorted me to the back seat in his ride. He introduced me to his driver and then we pulled off.

"So I hear you handle business for Rick?"

"You did, huh? I only handle business for myself," I lied.

"That's not true. I know your story. I know your every move."

Trent was staring at me.

"Oh yeah, so did you know I was going to do this?"

I leaned closer to him and planted a passionate kiss on him. He squirmed and then he relaxed as he got caught up in my trance. I tongued him softly while he gripped my ass tightly.

"Damn you a feisty little hot thing," He laughed as he came up for air.

~~~~~~~~~~

We arrived at Club Havana in Baltimore. We were meeting up with one of Trent's connects. We didn't see him right away so we danced a little bit. When Trent spotted his connect, we walked over to him and greeting him. Trent introduced me to Tiny, who was the total opposite of his name. He was Latino. He was about 6'3 and easily 350 pounds. He was a solid big boy and he was light on his feet.

"Can I have this dance, Ms.?" He pulled me on the dance floor.

Robin Thicke's *Everything I Can't Have* was playing and we danced the salsa to it. Tiny danced better than any smaller man I've danced with. He had me twirling and dipping with every rhythm of the song. He kept his eye on me like I was the prize.

We laughed and enjoyed each other's company. After we had drinks, Trent asked for our party to move outside. We stood outside on the sidewalk where we were waiting for valet to bring our cars.

"Are you following me?" Tiny asked Trent.

Tiny pulled out a gun and put it to Trent head. "Fuck no, little nigga! You can't be trusted." He pushed the barrel closer to his temple. "You didn't think I forgot about that set up you pulled on my mans and 'em did you?"

Trent's face showed no fear. I reached for the gun I had strapped to my thigh and pointed to the back of Tiny's head. Two shoots and I saw his big body hit the pavement. Loud screams and all types of commotion were coming from everywhere.

"That shit was crazy, ma!" Trent yelled. "We got get up outta here."

We dipped in between a few cars and left his ride with the drive. He called a cab to pick us up near the club.

My heart was racing. I couldn't believe I killed somebody. I kept hearing the shoots in my head. I kept seeing Tiny's big body fall before me. It was like the scene was on replay. My face went blank and I heard Trent asking was I cool. He wanted to know if the shit was alright with me. But I couldn't respond. I felt like I stepped out of my body looking down at myself. What the hell was I getting myself into? Killing someone was a guaranteed death sentence in the game. What the fuck? My head was spinning and I was astonished by my behavior. What the fuck happened to me?

Chapter Ten
Moni

Graduation was rolling around quickly. I was hurt to learn KeKey wasn't going to make it to my graduation. She had been out of town for almost two months. She rarely communicated with me unless it was her weekly text message to let me know she was doing ok.

I couldn't believe she finally decided to call me.

"I know you mad at me for a lot of reasons right now but I had to get away from Annapolis. These bitches were about to drive me crazy! I had to leave." KeKey sound as if she had been crying.

"Ke, is everything alright?" I questioned. "You sound so sad."

"I'm good, bitch!" She laughed. "You the one sounding all emotional."

"Yeah whatever. Are you pregnant, Ke? I've never heard you sound this way."

"No I'm not knocked up!" She spoke loudly.

"Then why you leave without one word?" I was getting in her business.

"You wouldn't understand. Sometimes you just need some space?"

"Where are you? When you coming home?" I knew she wish I'd let it go.

"I'm down in North Carolina with my aunt and uncle."

"What? I've never heard you talk about your family down in North Carolina."

"What you supposed to know my whole family?" She was mad.

"No, but I pretty much know your whole family except for this aunt and uncle you claiming you got down in North Carolina."

"Are you saying I'm lying?" she huffed.

"No, I'm just saying we best friends and I thought we were like sisters. So why wouldn't I know your family down south?"

"You don't know everything about me, Moni," she said after a long pause.

"Would you just come home and stop being stubborn?"

"Awe, you really missed me?"

"A little bit!" I said with excitement. "So get your butt on the road and come home."

"It might not be a good time to come back home. I might be too hot."

"I'm sure it's not as hot as North Carolina up here."

"No, dumb ass!" She laughed. "Some people might be after me."

"What? You are talking crazy now!"

"I'm serious, Moni. I told you, you really don't know shit about me. I did some fucked up shit and I'm scared to come home."

I took a deep breath and we listened to each other breathe for a little bit. I didn't know what KeKey did to think somebody was after her. I told her to stop running behind these little thugs before she got caught up. That's what happened when you lived by the streets.

I didn't get off the phone until KeKey agreed to come back home. She said she would lay low for a little while. That was my best friend so I would have her back with any drama that might come her way. I kept telling KeKey she was too old to be wilding out in the streets. Now she was scared to come back to the town she loved so much. I couldn't picture KeKey being away from Annapolis for too long. She loved the respect she got. She was one of the few chicks who were feminine and still rolled with the niggas like she was one of them. She was like a down ass chick. Half the girls from around the way feared her. The other half just couldn't stand her.

KeKey collected a lot of enemies being my protector. If a bitch looked at me wrong, she was up in their face like, *if you got beef with my girl, you got beef with me*. She would make me stand up for myself to the girls that used to hate on me around the way. Thinking back really had me missing her crazy ass. I couldn't wait until she got home.

~~~~~~~~

It was two weeks after I heard from KeKey. I was sitting over Rick's house when I heard a knock at the door. I walked to the door with one of his big t-shirts on. I looked out the peephole and I started screaming.

"Oh my God!" I opened the door. "When the hell you get home?"

"I got home this morning." We hugged each other. "I stopped by this morning but your car wasn't out front."

"Yeah, girl, I started a new job. I'm sorry!" I apologized for having KeKey standing at the door. "Girl, come in." I stepped a side and let her come inside.

"So where you working at now?"

"I work for this company that's located a few minutes from BWI. They paying good money, too. I was thinking about getting my own place."

"For what? If you not here, you out getting your hair done." She widened her eyes. "That would be a waste of money because you will still spend most of your time at Rick's. And what you worrying about making good money for? Rick make enough money for you to be set for life." She rolled her eyes.

"That's Rick's money. I still gotta make my money too."

Rick came into the living room and did a double take. "Where you been hiding at?"

"I had a family emergency."

"Yeah that's what they all say." He smiled.

"What you trying say?" She was anxious. "Rick, what you heard."

"I didn't hear shit. I'm just asking questions." Rick got smart with her.

KeKey rolled her eyes.

Rick and KeKey were developing a serious love/hate relationship. You could tell they had love for each other but they work each other's nervous like brother and sister. Every question Rick asked KeKey, she would get an attitude with him.

"So what made you come home?" Rick questioned while rolling up a blunt.

"Ain't shit make me come home. I just got tired of helping my aunt out. Plus I was missing my home girl, Moni."

She smiled at me.

"Oh, that's what it was?"

"Yeah, nigga!" She rolled her eyes.

I interrupted their conversation when I handed Rick his cell phone that was ringing. I didn't look at the display name to see who it was, but the look on Rick face showed it was serious business. He walked into the kitchen to take his call. KeKey was trying to eavesdrop but Rick was talking low.

"Let's make that shit happen," he spoke into the phone. When Rick returned to the living room, he walked over to me, and kissed me on my lips. "Baby, I'm about to make a run for a second. Lock up if you leave."

"Okay baby." I hugged him and watched him walk out the door.

"I wonder what that was all about?" KeKey was being nosy.

"Girl, I don't ask. I know that look! When business call, Rick goes running." KeKey just looked at me like she was upset to see Rick running out on me. "You hungry?" I changed the subject

"No. I ate before I got here."

"I'm hungry. You want ride out to get a bite to eat?"

"Yeah I'll go with you."

I was closed the door behind me after making sure everything was locked up, I watched KeKey climb into a wine color 2007 GMC Yukon.

"This ride is hot! Is this a rental?"

"No. I traded my ride in." She smiled.

"For real? Damn girl, how you afford it?"

"You know I get money."

"Yeah but that's some serious money right there. You don't even work."

"I keep telling you, you don't have to work to get that paper. That's what these hustling ass niggas for." She looked at me like she was schooling me. "You gotta get in them niggas head, fuck 'em good, then get that money! I know you don't think I had to work for this money." She moved her body like she was teaching me how to ride a dick. We were cracking up laughing.

We rode to the Harbour Center where we ended up eating at this little sub shop. We shared a foot long and got two drinks.

"Damn, Moni, I forgot how good these subs were."

"I know. I bet you didn't have anything like this down south."

"Not a sub like this but they threw down on the soul food down there."

"Oh for real?"

"Hell yeah! You got to go down there just for the food," KeKey told me.

Half way into our sub, KeKey got a phone call that had her looking like she seen a ghost.

"What the fuck you just say?" she screamed into the phone. "Somebody threw a bottle in my mother's window and what?" KeKey dropped the phone and fainted.

Chapter Eleven
Moni

"Someone please call 911!" I yelled when I saw KeKey fall to the floor. "Somebody help me!" I cried.

The man behind the stand quickly picked up the phone and made the emergency phone call. I shook KeKey several times and she didn't respond. She lay there looking pale in the face and breathless. I lifted her head up off the floor and placed in my lap.

"You're going to be okay." I moved her hair out of her face. "I'm not gonna leave you."

The ambulance arrived to the sub shop about ten minutes later. They asked me some questions and I climbed in the back with KeKey. On our way to the hospital, KeKey began blinking her eyes as she awake from her unconsciousness.

"Moni," she called.

"I'm here." I comforted her.

"Moni, everything is fucked up." She started crying. "I'm scared and I want to get out of here."

I never saw KeKey cry like that before. It made me cry too.

"You don't have to be scared. You just got a little bad news and fainted," I told her.

"You don't understand. I want to get up out of here. I feel fine now."

"No, the doctors have to check you out to be sure everything is alright."

She wasn't feeling the idea until the paramedic told her she could faint again and have some difficulties. She calmed down and didn't say another word. Tears were still falling from her eyes. She was silent during the quick ride to the hospital. Once we got a small room in the emergency room, KeKey dosed off from the medicine she was on. I kept putting my hand over her face to feel her breath. She wasn't able to tell me what all happened with her mother but I knew it was serious.

After being released from the hospital, we caught a cab to get KeKey's truck. The stores had closed except for the movie theater. When I paid the cab driver he opened the back door to let us out.

"Are you okay to drive?" KeKey shook her head no.

I took her keys from her and opened the doors. She went around to the passenger side and started flipping out.

"Oh my God!" She fell to her knees. "I can't believe this is happening to me!"

I ran to her side to see what happened and someone had spray painted:

You playing a grown man's game bitch!

"What did you do, KeKey?" I yelled.

"I did something fucked up and now they're gonna kill me. They killed my mother Moni. They threw a bottle in the house with gasoline and they spray painted the front door with the same message." She began crying again.

At first I was at a lost for words. My best friend was crying because her world was falling all around her. Her mother died in a fire that was meant for her. She was so paranoid that she didn't want to go visit her mother's body.

"KeKey, You have to go see your mother. You won't be able to live with yourself knowing you didn't do this," I tried to reason with her.

"I really don't think I'll live to see anything. They wanna kill me with no hesitations." She cried.

"Don't say that! You are just talking crazy."

"No I'm not," she yelled. "Stop always trying to butter every fucking thing up! I fucked up in a big way and I have to pay."

"Did you set up the wrong people KeKey?"

"No," She put her head down. "I killed a nigga."

I felt like my heart dropped in my stomach. I was astonished and I couldn't speak or move. I looked at KeKey like she was changing everyday.

She was turning into the female version of Rick. She was always chasing money and she didn't care who she hurt in the process of getting it. I felt like I didn't know her anymore. She wasn't that cool best friend that I once shared everything with and she did the same with me. I felt like she was no longer the girl I called my sister.

I turned my back to KeKey and began walking away. She was right, she was hot! I didn't want to be in the mix of her drama. Bullets didn't have a name on them and if those people wanted her dead, they wouldn't care who was around or who those bullets hit.

"Where are you going?" I heard her crying. "Please don't walk away from me."

"What do you mean don't walk away?" I yelled. "Isn't that what you always do? Walk away from shit?"

"I know you aren't playing me like this after all the fucked up shit Rick has done."

"Rick is open with his dirt. I know what he is about but you, you a sneaky ass bitch!"

"Oh really? I bet I wasn't a bitch when all them bitches were about to beat your ass!" She got in my face.

"I don't feel like I can trust you anymore. When you ready to be open with me, then I'll talk to you. If not, take your ass back to North Carolina with your pretend aunt."

It was the last I heard of KeKey for a long time. She didn't even stick around to see her mother get buried. She got out of Annapolis quickly. I didn't care where she went. I felt betrayed. She was always sneaking around and doing something grimy. I was pissed off with her. I knew she was hurting because we weren't talking and she lost her mother. Her mother was such a sweet heart. She had nobody in her life but sister. She walked away from her too.

KeKey must have done a lot of people dirty. She never talked to me about drugs or who she ran with. I was surprised she told me she killed somebody. I didn't know why she let herself get caught up with being a killer. She knew what was to come next. I thought the drug games were just a get money fast thing she was into. I didn't think she was in that deep. KeKey made me think twice about the drug game. I felt like I needed to distance myself from it entirely.

Chapter Twelve
Moni

I arrived at the office twenty minutes early and I ran into Jay, the cutie who slipped me his number in my psych class.

"Monet," he called for me. "I thought that was you." He spoke like cheerfully. His smile was so sexy.

"Hi Jay," I turned towards his voice. "What you doing up this way?"

"I just started a job in this building," he told me.

"On what floor?"

"The third floor."

"I'm on the second floor."

"That's what's up. That means I'm on top of you."

"Oh yeah!" We laughed together. "Not quite." I winked.

"You know what I meant. So what do you do on your job Monet?"

"I work in the CPA office of Berkley and Smith. I am their junior accountant."

"That's cool. I got a job at Money Management. Right now I'm a financial advisor."

"Oh really! That's what's up!" I smiled.

"So can I take you out for lunch?"

"You know I'm seeing someone right." I blushed.

"Yeah but I don't care about Rick." He searched my eyes. "The way I see it, he just gonna be around until he get locked up or die."

"Damn that's messed up to hear you say something like that," I said with an attitude.

"I'm serious, Monet. How many drug dealers you know who can retire and still sit pretty in a big house and nice ride?"

"He can save his money and start a legal business," I told him.

"Yeah that might work for some but don't you think the police will take that business too?"

"Not if he stop selling before the police have enough evidence to lock him up."

"Did you ever think they might already have enough?"

I didn't respond. I was thinking about what he was suggesting. Then he apologized.

"I don't mean to sound like I'm hating on him. I can see why you with him. You're protected. Nobody will fuck with you but what has it gotten you?"

"It got me a lot of money." Not speaking of the ass whopping I took from hating chicks and the dudes that robbed me.

"So I take it you're only into men that make a lot of money?"

"No. I haven't been with anyone other than Rick. I never thought about being with anyone else."

"Come on. You never pictured yourself with someone you have something in common with? Or someone you attracted to?"

"Yeah but I wouldn't act on it. I'm loyal to Rick," I proclaimed.

"So what you think about lunch?" he asked. "It will be very innocent."

I thought about it for a minute. I knew Rick would kill me if he knew I was even looking at another man the way I was looking at Jay. He was too sexy not to stare. I had to replay it in my mind. It will be innocent.

"Okay. I'll go as long as you don't talk about me and Rick."

"No problem. I'll meet you right here at noon." He was referring to the lobby of the building we worked in.

Jay practically skipped to the elevator door and pushed the button. I didn't want to ride up with him so I walked to the restroom on the lobby floor. I walked inside and looked in the mirror and noticed how much I was blushing at the thought of having lunch with another man.

I pretty much floated through the first four hours of work. I was on top of my job and ahead of schedule. Everyone was pleased with my work and my attitude. I felt like I was a new person. I was amazed at how Jay made me feel. Ten minutes before noon, I sat at my desk and did my count down. When the computer clock said 12:00 p.m., I put on some lip-gloss and then checked my hair and makeup.

I arrived in the lobby at five after noon. Jay was promptly waiting for me.

"Were you waiting long?"

"No, just five minutes."

"Look at you being on time."

"Yeah. That's what I do. I don't believe in CPT, colored people time," he laughed at his joke.

Jay walked over to me and grabbed my hand and led me out of the building. We walked to his black 2007 Chevy Impala and he opened the door for me. I reached over and pushed his door open for him. He smiled at me.

"You are so beautiful, Monet." He smiled.

"Thank you, Jay." I was smiling ear to ear.

We ate lunch, laughed, and joked about everything. We really enjoyed each other's company. Jay was very respectful and polite. We sat next to each other while we enjoyed our lunch. The waitress came to our table with more drinks and she complimented us.

"You two make a very nice couple. I think he just adores you."

"Thank you."

"Wow, sorry. I hope that didn't make you uncomfortable."

"Not at all. It was cool."

"Good."

I was sad when I realized it was time to get back to work. When the waitress returned with the check, I offered to pay it.

"I will not let you pay for lunch, girl, so put your purse away," he told me.

"It's cool. I got this."

"No you don't. I do." He gave the waitress his credit card and he smiled at me.

"Okay, big pimping."

Once we got in his car, Jay pushed a button to change his disc. He started the latest Raheem Devaughn CD.

"I love this CD. I play it all day long."

"Oh yeah. I like it too."

We started singing along with the songs and laughing when we didn't know all the words. Once we got back to our office building, he opened my door again and helped me out of the car. He kissed my hand and then stared at me.

"Did I tell you how beautiful you are Monet?"

"No you didn't," I lied.

"You are absolutely stunning."

"Thank you again."

I had that big, cheesy grin.

"So I know you have a man in all but I really would like to take you on a date."

"I can't do that." I really didn't want to say that.

"Why? Didn't you enjoy today?"

"Yes but Rick will find out."

"So. I'm willing to take that chance."

"I'm not. Do you know what he does to people who betray him?"

"I don't care," he stated.

"I do, Jay. I'm sorry."

"How about we go out of state?"

"Out of state? Where?"

"Jersey."

"Atlantic City?"

"Anywhere you want to go."

"Okay," I agreed. "I look forward to it."

By mid week, I started missing talking to Jay so I got another cell phone that I hid so Rick couldn't go through it. Jay was the only person that had the number. When Rick went on a run, I was on the phone talking to Jay. Sometimes we would send text messages if Rick was around. I would go into the bathroom to respond to his messages.

Since the beginning of the week, Jay and I had been on three lunch dates. On Friday, he surprised me with a beautiful bouquet of assorted color roses. They were waiting at my desk for me when I arrived to work. Normally Jay would walk me to the office but he wasn't in the lobby that morning. I had gotten used to seeing him every morning. He was always excited to see me and I was excited to see him, too.

After admiring the roses and getting settled at my desk, I called Jay to thank him for the roses.

"You are too much, Jonathan Jackson."

"What are you talking about?"

"I'm talking about the beautiful roses you got me. They are so beautiful. Thank you." I smiled while staring at the roses.

"You're most welcome, Monet. So tell me, are the roses as beautiful as you are?"

"Not at all."

"I was feeling some kind of way this morning when I didn't see you in the lobby," I told him.

"Really? I was wondering where you were."

"I was trying to get to your desk before you did. At first the secretary wasn't trying to let me in your office. She was like, leave it here."

"Yeah, she can be that way sometimes."

"I don't know why. She sees me everyday with you."

"Just doing her job I suppose."

"Doing it a little too well if you as me."

"Tonight is the night," changing the subject. "Are you excited?"

"Yes I am. I've been looking forward to spending time with you since we met at college," he admitted.

"You'll get that chance tonight."

"We could've been had this chance if you didn't throw my number away."

"I couldn't chance Rick finding it."

"I figured that much." He sighed. "So what will you tell him so you can get away?"

"I don't need to tell him anything. He will be out of town this weekend. He's going to Philly." I was excited.

"He always out of state. Doesn't he know you shouldn't leave treasures in a glass house?"

"I guess not. He might think no one is brave enough to touch his treasures." I giggled.

"He must be dumb if he thinks that."

After we got off the phone, I got started on my work. Most of the staff didn't arrive in the office until nine. I still had about thirty minutes to myself but I jumped right into my deadlines. I was looking over some documents on my desk when my cell phone vibrated on my desk.

"Hello," I answered.

"Hey, princess," Rick said. "Sorry I didn't make it back home before you went to work."

"No problem. I didn't stay up too long after you left." I was lying.

"I thought you looked a little tired. I wanted to remind you that I'ma be out of town this weekend."

"Yeah I remembered. I guess I'm not invited on this trip."

"No, baby. I wouldn't get you involved in a trip like this. It's not for a woman. Not my princess anyway."

"I understand," I lied.

"Good. I'll see you when I get back. Love you, shawty."

"Love you, too."

When we got off the phone, I started calculating in my mind how many trips I wasn't invited to. I wondered what type of drug business needed to be handled for the whole weekend. What was really going on with Rick? He always had some slick game. I almost didn't care what he was doing because I wanted to spend time with Jay. I didn't care anymore about feeling guilty for spending time with Jay because Rick was playing me. He must have thought I was dumb. All the late night business issues and some grown ass man not being able to handle business by themselves. I push those thoughts aside because I was not gonna be sitting at home waiting on Rick to come home.

Chapter Thirteen
Rick

KeKey thought she was a ride or die bitch until Tiny's crew put that to a test. She ran like a little bitch. I was surprised to see her sitting in my living room like she didn't have niggas looking for her. I was offered $25,000 to kill her ass. Them niggas contacted me because they knew she was part of my crew. Word got around that I lost trust in her. I walked away from the offer.

I didn't want that type of shit around my house. I didn't want it around Moni either. She never was good when it came to picking her friends. I ran through almost all her crew. Steph was the only one I didn't holla at. I thought she was manlier than most niggas I ran with but Moni swore she was strictly dickly. KeKey was on my dick too hard. She wanted to go on every run with me. She thought she was a lieutenant or some shit. She got too cocky in the business. I started distancing myself from her and distancing her from the game.

This little shawty from Bywater name Taneka rolled with me to Philly. I was fucking with her the night before and I asked her to roll out with me. She was down. I picked her up around noon so we wouldn't run into any traffic. I dropped her off at a little rental car spot and she got us a blue 2007 Explorer. She picked me up from my house and then we got on the road. She drove while I sat back and listened to some music.

"I never did anything like this." She told me. She was excited.

"Like what?"

"I never fucked with any niggas that get money like you Rick."

"Oh yeah." I laughed. "I guess you never been with a real hustler."

"No but I always wanted to fuck you," licking her lips.

"Oh shit! That's what's up shawty."

"My momma would kill me if she knew what I was doing or if she knew I was with you." She laughed. "She always talking bad about dealers."

"You're mom can trust you with me." I told her.

"I doubt she would. You like eight years older than me and you sling more drugs than a little bit." She glanced at me. "Plus, I'm supposed to be working the summer job she got me."

"I'll give you the money you missed out on from work. How 'bout that?"

"For real? That's so cool." She smiled.

I watched her pop open the CD case and put Jay-Z volume 3 CD in the CD loader.

"This CD is fire. Thank you for getting it for me."

"It wasn't nothing. I got this CD in my car and at my crib." I smiled. "What your young ass know about that nigga Jay-Z?"

"I know a little som'in."

I loved the young bitches. They didn't want too much. A pair of Nikes and a CD then she sucked me off like I paid her mother's rent or something.

It didn't take long before we arrived to Philly. I was meeting up with this nigga name Trent at Franklin Mills mall. I peeled off two hundred dollar bills and handed them to Taneka.

"I'm gonna go take care some business and I'll meet you back right here." I was referring to the food court. "See you in an hour."

"Okay Rick." She leaned in to kiss me.

I watched her walk away with her phat ass bouncing. Taneka's body was nicer than some grown woman I've came across. She was thick like I like 'em. I loved watching her walk away. Her ass was round and wide with a thin waist. She always put a little switch in her walk when she knew I was watching.

Trent and I did an exchange for money and drugs. I gave him a briefcase full of Franklin faces and he gave me one full of cocaine. I opened the briefcase and looked at the product to make sure it was all there.

"We straight?"

"Hell yeah nigga," I shook his hand. "Nice doing business with you."

"No doubt. Next time you in town, hit a nigga up," He smiled.

"No doubt, nigga. No doubt."

We went our separate ways. After taking care of business. I went back to the food court where Taneka was waiting for me. She had four shopping bags in her hands. She got a pair of shoes, a bracelet from a cheap jewelry stand, and some clothes.

"Look what I got." She came running up to me.

"I 'on't see anything in them bags for me." I teased.

"You didn't give me enough money."

"I see you were only thinking about you. That's fucked up."

"No I wasn't. I saw this cute shirt for you but it was ninety dollars and I had already spent too much money to get it."

"I was fucking with you shawty." I laughed. "You didn't have to get me anything."

She took her gum out her mouth and tongued me down. "How you like that?"

"I'd like it better shawty if you did that to my dick."

"I will when we get in the truck."

"I can't wait that long. Hook my shit up right now." I smiled at her.

"Pull it out." She giggled.

I grabbed her bags out her hand and we walked over to a table. I put the bags on the floor next to my foot and she got underneath the table. The bags blocked what she was doing on one side but she was visible on another. Once she got comfortable under the table, she started fumbling around in my pants until she pulled my rock hard dick out. She deep throated my dick slowly. She had me grabbing for the sides of the table when she ran her tongue up and down my dick. She nibbled and pulled at the head for a little before she deep throated it again. She continued with her routine for almost ten minutes until I came. She started squeezing my balls when I was coming to make me come faster. She let me squirt in her mouth until I was dry. Now that's what I called a bad bitch.

Chapter Fourteen
Moni

Jay and I arrived at the Caesar's casino and hotel about nine p.m. I started getting nervous being with him. He made me feel so good like how Rick once did. Jay opened my door and I stepped out looking sexy in a white halter dress and white high heel sandals.

"Stunning, Ms. Monet." He smiled.

"Thank you."

He took my hand and led me into the casino. Our eyes lit up once we saw all the different games we could play. First I sat at a slot machine and Jay looked at me like I was crazy.

"Have you ever been here before?"

"No. Why?"

"You can't win big at that slot machine. You gotta play something bigger," he suggested.

"I'm not trying to lose my money. I would like to leave with the clothes on my back."

"Okay well stay right here. I'ma go hit up the crap table." He pointed in the direction of the crap tables.

After losing forty dollars in the slot machine, I was ready to quit. I was looking around for Jay and then I heard a lot of applauding and yelling over at one of the crap tables. I walked over and Jay was handling his business. He was rolling them dice something serious. He let me blow on them for good luck. When he hit another seven, he hugged me tightly.

"I knew you were good luck."

He kissed me on my forehead. He turned towards the tall blonde lady carrying drinks and waved for her to come over to him.

"Can I get you a drink?"

"Yes, please. Get me an Absolute and cranberry juice for the beautiful lady and a Long Island ice tea for me," he told her.

"Right away sir." She walked away as she flipped her long hair over her shoulder.

When she returned, Jay swallowed down his drink fast. I looked at him like his chest had to be on fire.

"You ok, baby?"

"Yeah. That drink was weak."

"Blow 'em one more time, momma."

"There you go, baby." I blew his dice.

Jay hit so many sevens in a row, one of the casino managers asked him if he was spending the night.

"We didn't plan on it."

"Well you might as well because I have a complimentary room for our big winner."

I guess the manager didn't want to see that kind of money leave the casino.

"Oh yeah! I'll take that." He looked at me. "If it's ok with you."

"Sure." I thought about it briefly. I wasn't expecting Rick to be home anytime soon. Why not have a little fun while he was away? After three hours of gambling, we got our key to the room and then we got on the elevator to go upstairs. I leaned my head on Jay's chest. I was a little tired.

"I can't believe you won all that money." I smiled. "Are you gonna play again." I yarned.

"Hell no. I'm taking my money with me."

"I'm hungry. I hope room service still taking orders." I felt a rumble in my stomach and I rubbed it.

"They should be. If not, we can run out to get a bit to eat," he offered.

"No, I'm too tired to leave out."

"Okay baby."

Jay unlocked the door to our room and to my surprise, the room was well lit from candle lights.

"Oh my!" He faked being surprised. "We must have the wrong room." His smile was so big, there was no way he could fake it.

"Don't play dumb Jay." I laughed. "When did you do this?"

I walked over to the table that had a big candle in the center. There was a bottle of champagne chilling on a bucket of ice to the left side of the table. It was a very big tray of food covered with a big silver lid to keep it hot. I pulled the lid off the tray and uncovered two plates of steak, mashed potatoes, and mixed

79

veggies. There was a small bowl of dinner rolls in between the plates.

"When did you have time to do this?"

"When I cashed out my tickets."

"You are so good to me." I hugged him.

"This is just the beginning." He pulled out my seat for me and motioned for me to sit down.

"Thank you, Jay."

"You're welcome beautiful lady." He kissed my hand.

He sat across from me and bowed his head to bless our food. I was shocked because I never been around a man that prayed. I bowed my head and closed my eyes.

"Father, God I thank you for bringing Monet into my life. I ask you to watch over the both of us as we enjoy our trip. I ask you to please forgive anything that we have done or will do that is unlike you." He paused. "I ask you to bless the cook who has prepared this food for us as well. In Jesus name, Amen."

"Amen."

Jay's brief blessing really surprised me. In our house as a kid, God was only mentioned during Easter and Christmas. My sister and I ate our meals in front of the TV and the rest of the family ate whenever. So grace wasn't a big part of growing up either.

After enjoying our very late dinner, Jay walked over to the miniature refrigerator to pull out a tray and then he returned back to the table.

"I hope you got space for these," He said as he sat down the tray of chocolate covered strawberries.

"These are my favorite." I reached for a strawberry.

"I hope to be a part of your list of favorites too." He winked.

"You already are." I blushed.

"So you like me more than the strawberries?"

"Not yet. Give me another day."

I ate three strawberries on top of dinner. I was stuffed and ready to fall asleep.

"I wish I had known we were staying so I could have brought something to sleep in."

"Here, you can sleep in this." Jay took off his button up shirt and gave me his wife beater.

"What will you sleep in?"

"I can sleep in my boxers."

I took his shirt and took it in the bathroom to change out of my dress. When I returned, Jay was folding his pants and laid them on the chair. I pulled back the covers on the bed and crawled in.

"Come here." Jay pulled me close to him.

"Yes." I smiled.

"I've been waiting a long time for this." He stared at me with those sexy eyes. He grabbed me by my chin and kissed me softly. I was so lost in his kiss. It was full of passion. I pulled away when I felt myself getting excited. "Did I move do fast?"

"No. The kiss was right on point." I enjoyed it.

Jay kissed me again and I didn't pull away. We tasted each other's tongues and licked each other's lips. He pulled me on top of him while he rubbed my back and ran his fingers through my hair. I looked into his eyes and I felt like I was floating on a cloud. Jay wrapped his arms around me and I fell asleep listening to his heartbeat.

The sun rise woke me out of my sleep. I rolled away from Jay so I could get out of the bed. When Jay felt me move, he rolled over and pulled me back into his arms.

"Where you think you going?" He spoke in his sleepy voice.

"I'm not going anywhere. I just wanted to get up and go into the bathroom."

"Oh sorry. Go ahead." He moved his arm.

I went into the bathroom and washed my face and brushed my teeth. When I returned, Jay was getting off the phone with room service.

"I hope you like your eggs scrabbled."

"Yes I do, with cheese."

"Good, that's exactly how I ordered them."

I sat next to Jay and I reached for his hand and then put it in my lap.

"I really enjoyed our trip together." I sighed. "I wish it didn't have to end but we both know Rick will be home soon and I fear what he might do to you if he found out about us."

"I can't walk away from you now. It's too late. I already care for you. I can't stand seeing you in a relationship with someone who doesn't deserve you." He gave me a really deep sincere look.

"I don't wanna be with him anymore but I'm scared of leaving him. He might try hurting me or something worse."

"Don't think like that, Monet. You have to speak up to Rick. He is only a man. He isn't God."

"He thinks he is."

Our conversation was interrupted by a knock at the door. "Room service," the man announced.

We ate our food in bed. Jay ordered us eggs, bacon, grits, and French toast. We enjoyed the rest of the strawberries from the night before and then we took a quick nap before getting back on the road. I had so much fun with Jay. He was like a gift from God and an escape from Rick and his foul life. Although it was hard to walk away from all the money Rick gave me, I knew with Jay, I wouldn't be fighting or ducking bullets.

I loved Rick because he was good to me. He gave me what I wanted and a lot of things I didn't need. He was my first love so I couldn't let another bitch have him. Then, when I thought about it, he probably already had half of Annapolis. He didn't care who he hurt in the process of doing his thing. I wished it were an easy way out of our relationship.

When I woke from my nap, my cell phone was ringing non-stop.

"You might wanna get that," Jay said. "It rung like six times already."

"Really? That's strange."

I picked up my phone and it had six missed calls and six new messages. I didn't recognize the number so I looked at it for a second. Then I called it back.

"Hello. Did someone call this number?"

"Moni! It's you're boy, Ace. Sorry to wake you."

"It's cool. Is everything okay?"

"No. I take it you didn't hear?"

"Hear what?"

I almost dropped the damn phone when I heard what happened. I was standing there staring out in space while trying to take in what I was just informed of.

Chapter Fifteen
Rick

Taneka wasn't in a rush to get back home but I was missing Moni, my little princess. I watched Taneka carry herself like she was queen bee up in Philly. She was checking bitches quick if she thought they were checking me out. Some niggas might think a jealous bitch was cool and shit but not me. I hated seeing Taneka act like a straight up hood rat. This little high yellow, skinny chick smiled at me when we were leaving out of a bar together and then she whispered something to her friend that made them giggle.

"I know you better get them fucking eyes off my man before I snatch 'em out your damn head, trick!" Taneka was loud and ignorant. She rolled her eyes.

"Excuse me?" high yellow said.

"You're fucking excused, bitch."

The chick stepped to Taneka like she was about to handle her business and her friend had her back. I stepped in between the women and I apologized to high yellow.

"It's cool, but next time I might have to tap that bitch ass if I see her again." She looked her up and down like she dared her to say something.

"Oh really?" Taneka yelled. "I'll be waiting for that shit."

"Why you acting like a little ass girl?" I pulled her away from the crowd of people forming.

"She was disrespecting me." Her eyes widened.

"No you disrespected yourself." It definitely wasn't a good look for her.

Taneka folded her arms and looked at me like she didn't believe I was questioning her behavior. She didn't have anything else to say. I couldn't wait to drop her young ass off when we got back to town.

We walked to our ride and about ten minutes of silence, Taneka apologized for her behavior.

"Are you mad at me, Rick?"

"No I'm not mad. I think you coulda handled the situation differently though." I looked at her. "That shit was childish."

"Okay cool. It won't happen again."

She was right because I didn't see me taking her on a run with me ever again.

"Good." I said to her before finding some music on the radio.

"How about I make it better?" she said while pulling at my belt.

"You must really like this dick, huh?"

"Yeah. Take it out so I can taste it."

She sucked me off before we got back on the Interstate to head home. Taneka got comfortable in her seat by adjusting it so she could lay back and go to sleep. I looked at her and wished I had asked her to drive back to town. I was feeling tired too, but I sucked that shit up and kept driving. I was turning on to 495 when I saw the bright lights and heard the sirens.

"Oh shit!" I panicked. "Taneka, get the fuck up!"

She woke up and squinted her eyes from all the bright lights. "Oh shit, Rick. What the fuck we gon' do?"

"Stay cool, shawty."

"Is the car dirty?" She asked on the verge of tears.

"No. I let that shit head to Maryland on the train," referring to the coke.

"Oh ok. What should I say?"

"Don't say nothing!"

I put on my calm face but I could've shit a brick when the police officer walked up to the driver side window.

"Mr. Richard Baker, please turn off the engine and place your hands on the steering wheel." The officer ordered.

"Is there a problem officer?" While following his instructions.

"Yes."

Then Trent walked up next to him. I almost went off on his ass but I had to keep my cool. Trent was dressed in a dark gray suit looking like the police more than the first time we met. When I first saw him, he had on a white t-shirt and a pair of jeans.

"Mr. Baker, let me introduce you to agent Banks."

Trent looked at me as if he was laughing at me.

"Mr. Rick Baker, pleased to meet you." He smiled.

"Nice to meet you."

"Mr. Baker, I understand you made a big purchase of cocaine from agent Banks. Is that true?"

"I don't know what you talking about," I lied.

"Of course you do." He was serious.

They pulled Taneka and myself from the ride and read us our rights. I felt like I was in a bad movie. How the fuck I let this shit happen. I knew Trent didn't seem like a nigga I could trust. He was selling his coke for too cheap when I thought about it. I knew I shouldn't have hollered at a nigga that said he was cool with KeKey. That bitch probably set my ass up.

After stuffing us in the back of a police car, they took us to the station. Taneka was released after Trent gave a statement saying she had nothing to do with the transaction. So then her mother came to pick her up. My ass was sitting in a cell mad at the world really fucking wishing I didn't take that drive to Philly.

My first phone call was to my lawyer. It was four o'clock in the morning when I interrupted his sleep.

"Kyle Busch speaking." He answered in his sleepy voice.

"Busch, wake that ass up!" I demanded.

"Rick, please tell me you aren't locked up in Philly!" he yelled into the phone.

"I wish I could fucking tell you that shit but it would be a lie."

"I was hoping the caller ID was playing tricks on me!" He yelled. "What the fuck, Rick! Didn't I just make some charges disappear a year ago?" He sounded like he was ready come through the phone and kill me.

"Yeah but ..."

"There are no buts when you're sitting in jail," he told me.

"I feel you. I'll take care of you for whatever you can do to make sure I don't spend the night here."

"It's Sunday. You will definitely be spending the night."

"Fuck man! Get up here ASAP!"

A female's voice interrupted our phone call telling me I had two minutes left to end my phone call.

"I will do my best. Do you need me to contact anyone?"

"Contact my man Ace and then tell him get a message to Moni." Before I could say anything else to my lawyer, the phone call disconnected.

I felt pissed off and defeated. When I was rushed back to my cell I started thinking about everything that happened. I couldn't believe I trusted Trent's bitch ass. I wanted to find the connection between him and KeKey's scandalous ass. I hoped she knew I wouldn't let it rest until I found out who was snitching. I was too mad to sleep or talk to the man I shared the cell with. The clock was moving real slow. I was trying to take my mind off the thoughts of wanting to kill Trent and KeKey. My body was full of rage and I couldn't get the thoughts out of my mind.

It was around noon when an officer called my name to tell me I had visitors. He escorted me to a little room where Busch was waiting for me.

"Did Ace come with you?"

"Good to see you too Rick."

"My bad Busch. Thank you for coming all the way out here on a fucking Sunday."

"You're welcome." He sat across from me. "Ace is in the waiting area."

"Cool. Did he get in touch with Moni?"

"Yes he did but she wasn't able to make it. She wasn't in town when Ace contacted her."

"Where the fuck she at?"

I was fuming.

"No one knows."

"Oh ok. We gon' have to talk about that shit."

"Listen Rick, Monet's whereabouts should be the last of your concerns. You're sitting in here behind bars and for what? What happened to you staying out the drug exchange?"

"KeKey used to take care of it for me but she's MIA. She told me about the nigga Trent and he turned out to be fucking Feds." I raised my voice.

"I don't care about your fucking operation Rick. Tell me why you told me you would get your shit straight?"

"I know Busch. I fucked up."

"Ok well let's start from the top. Tell me what you think they know about you."

I started from the beginning and at the end. Busch sat there looking like he could beat my ass.

"I know I fucked up. I promise if you fix this shit, I'll walk away from it all."

"You said that shit last time when I magically made shit disappear."

Busch was disappointed in me. Last time I got busted with some drug charges, he did his dirty work and paid off a lot of dirty cops. He paid witnesses to say they didn't see or hear shit. I hoped he still had that pull. I didn't know how strong his pull would be though. Those charges were in Maryland and now I faced Federal charges. The whole fucked up situation had me second-guessing if the drug game really was for me or should I just step down.

Chapter Sixteen
Moni

We were on our way to Maryland when Jay and I got in an argument. I felt like I needed to be there for Rick while he was sitting in jail but Jay couldn't see why.

"I don't understand what you possibily could do for Rick while he's sitting behind bars."

"Just the thought of knowing I'm there I guess." I stared at him.

"What?" He looked at me like I was crazy. "He won't know you're there. It's not as if they will let you stay in the waiting area until he goes to court. Jail isn't like a hospital." Jay was trying to make his point.

"I know but he might be mad that I wasn't there for him."

"So what do you want me to do? Drop you off at the jail?"

"No. I wouldn't ask you to do that."

"Monet, there's nothing you can do but wait until his hearing."

On the ride home I was quiet. I knew Rick was braver than I was but I felt like I needed to be there to protect him. He hadn't spent more than a few hours in jail so I didn't know how he was doing. I couldn't believe he got arested. He was always so careful. I was started to get mad at him for thinking he was untouchable.

After I got the thoughts of Rick out of my mind, I reached over and put my hand on Jay's. He smiled at me and then kissed my hand.

"I'm sorry for letting my emotions get the best of me earlier. I do understand what you were saying."

I smiled at him.

"You don't have to apologize. You are allowed to voice your opinion."

"Thank you. Next time, you can come right out and tell me when I'm thinking without using my brain."

"I can't do that. You are already emotional, I wouldn't want to make you cry."

I leaned over and gave Jay a kiss on his cheek. I continued to hold his hand while he was driving. We were our happy selves all over again. Everytime I looked into Jay's eyes, he made everything better. He took away any bad mood I was having.

"What are you over there blushing about?" He smiled showing off his sexy smile.

"You. You make me blush."

"Good to know beautiful."

My cell phone started ringing and it was from a blocked caller. I thought it was from the jail Rick was at. When I answered, it definitely wasn't Rick.

"Hello." I waited for a response.

"Yeah is this Moni?"

"Yeah this is she."

"I thought you should know Rick got locked up this morning."

"Yes I am aware. Who is this?"

"This Taneka. You might not know me but I was with him when he got locked up."

"I don't think I know you. So why are you calling me?

"Yeah, I thought you wouldn't know. I guess you not good at keepin' ya nigga happy." She laughed. "I wanted you to know who Rick has been spending his time with."

"Why you trying throw shit in my face?"

"I just thought you should know while you all laid up with your man when he gets home, don't forget he was spending money on me and fucking me all weekend." She bragged.

"So what did he buy you?" I asked. "Did you get a new car? Did you get a college degree? Did you get a bank roll of money for pocket change?" She didn't say anything. "I thought not, lil' miss trick! You were just something for the weekend. Nothing special."

I hung up before she could respond. I was so mad that I was blowing steam. "I hate a little scandalous ass bitch!" I raised my voice.

"Who was that girl?"

"This bitch that called to tell me she was spending the weekend fucking Rick and spending his money." I rolled my eyes. "He always fucking with little stank bitches and then he get all defensive when I question him about them."

"You are too good for that Monet."

"I know. I don't know why he always disrespecting me. He got bitches laughing at me everytime they see me because they seen him with somebody else."

I was trying to fight back my tears but I couldn't stop them. One rolled down my cheek.

"Monet, please don't cry." Jay wiped the tear from my face.

"I'm sorry. I'm so mad because I was so concerned about Rick being locked up. Now, I could care less. He could die there as far as I care."

"You don't mean that. You are just upset."

"No! I'm more than upset. Rick's always calling me his princess and telling me how special I am. He doesn't care about me. He just doesn't want anybody else to have me."

"Monet, you are a special woman. You deserve a lot more than Rick. You might be a princess to him but to me, you're a queen."

Jay turned my frown upside down. He always knew what to say to make it all better.

"Thank you." I leaned over to kiss him.

When I got back to Maryland, I was debating leaving Rick's home or staying. I didn't want to be there when he got out of jail but I didn't want to move back into my mother's house because there was no room for me. I had to suck it up and get a place of my own.

I went back to Rick's place and layed on the living room floor while going through pictures of us he had in a photo album on his book shelf. I smiled at the ones that brought back good memories but it didn't take long before I was balled into a fetal position crying. I felt like I wasted so much time dealing with Rick, his cheating, and the drug dealing. I guess that's the price you had to pay being Rick's princess.

The price of being his princess was not knowing if my man was coming home or going to jail. I didn't know if he was coming home or laid up with a bitch that wanna take your place. i might blink too long and somebody could rob me. All my man's enemies become my own. I had to duck bullets and fight the jealous bitches over my man. After all the bullshit I put up with, I didn't want the title anymore. I was taking my crown off.

Chapter Seventeen
Moni

When Rick got locked up, I took the following Monday off from work to be there for him. I rode to Philly with Ace and Mr. Busch for Rick's bail review. Jay sent me a text message asking me to keep him posted and call him when I get back to Maryland. I told him that I would when I was available.

When Rick saw Ace and I together, he gave us a little smile and turned back towards the judge. After some fast taking, Busch convinenced the judge to let Rick go on bail. It was set at 100k. I thought that was a lot of money but Busch pulled out his check book and wrote a check. I knew Ace must have put money in Busch's account because he couldn't be banking money like that on a regular. Then again, Busch was well known for handling high profile criminal cases. He probably get paid in large stacks of money to make all those charges disappear.

After Rick was free to go, he walked up to me and pulled me into his arms.

"I missed you so much princess."

"Yeah I bet. Did you miss Taneka, too?" I looked him up and down.

"Who the fuck is Taneka? Stop talking that bullshit girl!" He smiled trying to cover his lie.

"No, you stop talking bullshit Rick. Taneka called me and told me all about your weekend trip."

"You keep listening to these lying ass bitches. You gon' end up just like them. With nothing." He warned.

"Oh really? Well let me give you these right now so I won't need nothing else from you," I told him.

I reached into my purse and handed Rick my keys to the car and his house. He wouldn't take them.

"Get that shit out my face. What you leaving me now?"

"Yes I am. I already got my shit out your house last night."

"Where you think you going? You know you love me Moni. Stop playing games."

"You're the one getting fucked all weekend by the little bitch from the hood."

"Come here." He grabbed me and took me away from his friends. "Don't leave Monet. You know I need you."

He rarely called me Monet. He was feeling vulnerable and didn't know how to handle it. He put his head down and grabbed my hand.

"I know I fucked up Moni but I didn't mean to hurt you." He looked at me and searched my eyes.

"You always say that." I was hurting but I fought back the tears. "You keep talking the same shit over and over."

"I mean it this time. I promise." He hugged me. "You're my heart."

"Rick, I'm moving on." I pulled away and handed him the keys.

"At least keep this." He gave me back the car keys. "As a gift." He looked crushed.

"I don't need your car. I'll get a new one."

"No. I gave it to you and I want you to keep it. I told you I would look out for you. You don't ever have to ask for anything."

"I don't know how possible that might be with your drug bust."

"Busch gon' work that shit out. Trust me." He grabbed my chin and leaned in to kiss me. I pulled back while tears poured down my face.

"You and your lawyer don't have pull in Philly. This shit is Federal. You need to take it seriously." I told him. "You really need to let the game go Rick!"

"I will. I'ma lay low for a little bit. I promise."

"Okay so when you gone start?"

"As soon as we get home."

"That's all good but I'm not going home with you." I looked him in his eyes. "This shit ain't for me. I need security and a drama free life. I can't have that with you."

"Let's start over. I promise you I'll make shit right between us."

"It's too late. Just let it be what it is. It's over."

I walked away from him. I walked up to Busch's car where him and Ace were waiting for us. Rick caught up with me. He stood there while I open and close my door. *Jay would have opened and closed the door for me*, I thought. I smiled when I thought of how wonderful Jay treated me but part of me was nervous about him. In the beginning of Rick's and my relationship, I thought he was so good to me but now I've gotten wiser. I knew Rick wasn't good for me and I should've let him and his games go a long time ago. I was scared to make the same mistakes with Jay. I didn't want to be floating on cloud nine and then years later, realize I should have let him go too.

I knew Rick and Jay were totally different men and I probably shouldn't compare the two of them but Rick was my first and only love. I had nothing else to compare a man too. I didn't have a strong father figure in my life. My brothers weren't good examples of men. The thought left me lost and uncertain.

When we arrived to Rick's house where my car was parked, he asked me to walk in the house with him for a second. Ace plopped down on the couch and started surfing channels on the TV. I followed Rick into his bedroom.

"Are you sure you want to leave?"

"Yeah Rick. I still love you but I have to do me. I have to find out what I want out of life and how I'm gonna get what I want."

"I can understand that. You will always be my princess." He smiled at me.

"I know." I smiled.

He walked into his closet and then came back after moving stuff around. He handed me a knot of money.

"Take this. I don't want to ever see you struggle."

"I don't need this money. I will be alright." I fingered though the money and handed it to him.

"I'm not taking it back so take it. Its 50k right there. You gon' be set with it."

"I don't know what to say, Rick." I was jumping up and down on the inside.

I knew I should have walked away from the drug money but come on. Money was money. With money, you got a whole lot of shit that a broke person could only dream about.

"Don't say nothing. That's for all the fucking up I did. It's my pay back for you putting up with my shit." He grinned.

I put the money in my purse and then I lay with Rick until we fell asleep. Rick never slept long so by the time I woke up, him and Ace were gone. I was concerned that he might be out handling business as if nothing happened. I huffed at the thought and then thought about the big stack of money in my purse. On my way out, I ran to the car like I stole something. I had to rush to the bank with the money because I feared I would get robbed again.

After leaving the bank, I drove to Columbia and looked at a few apartments. I needed to get a place soon. My sister helped me put my stuff in my mother's basement the night before but I didn't want to leave it there too long. My sister and my niece were living there until she finished getting her house built down in southern Anne Arundel County.

After realizing the apartments in the area were pretty expensive, I decided to find a realtor. To my surprise, the lady was available at a new home. She just got finished with an open house walk-in with some potential clients. The house was in Crofton and it looked like a dollhouse from the outside. It was a white, three-level, single family home. The driveway was big and there was a garage. The basement was finished like my mom's. It could be another house down there. I fell in love instantly.

"I want this house right now. What do I have to do to move in right away?"

"You can't just move in, Ms. Harrison. You will have to find a lender and have the house inspected first."

"Okay. Get me a lender and tell them I'll pay cash for all expenses."

"Really?" Her eyes were widen.

"Yes. I don't want anyone take this house from me."

"If someone is ready to purchase this home, I will have to sell it."

I went into my purse and counted off ten crisp one hundred dollar bills and handed them to the realtor.

"Make it work, please."

"Not a problem." She smiled.

She got on the phone with a lender and ran outside to put the sold sign in the front yard. When she returned she reached for my hand to shake it.

"I look forward to handling business for you Ms. Harrison."

"Thank you. I look forward to hearing from you soon." I was excited.

I did my last walk through and left out. On my way out, I called Jay.

"You won't believe what I'm doing?" I almost jumped up and down.

"What are you doing beautiful?"

"Walking through my future house. Can you believe it? I'm so excited."

"I can hear that, baby. I'm happy for you too. So where are you on your way too?"

"To your apartment if you're there."

"I'm on my way back home. I had to pick up something for dinner."

"Okay cool. I'll see you soon."

"Okay."

I arrived at Jay's apartment twenty minutes later. He had dinner waiting for me when I got in. After dinner, he ran a bubble bath for me and then gave me a full body massage.

"Why are you so romantic?"

"Because I grew up with a group of romantic men. My father is romantic and so are all of my brothers."

"How many brothers do you have?"

"Five. I'm the middle child."

"Wow. I know your mom must have gone crazy with a house full of men."

"Not really. We all love and admire our mother the way our father did. I think that's why we're so caring with women. Both of my older brothers are married and have been happy for more than ten years."

"That seems unheard of." I laughed. "The divorce rate is climbing by the minute."

"You have to believe that it can last for it to actually work." He continued to rub my body.

Jay and I had an evening full of interesting conversations about his family, his past loves, and my family. He was definitely someone I could see myself falling in love with but not yet.

Chapter Eighteen
Moni

Five days after finding my dream house, I was moving in. It was early Saturday morning when my sister Vicky, her boyfriend and Jay came over to help me get settled in. Luckily, I didn't have anything heavy to move in. I purchased all new furniture for the whole house. I furnished one of my three rooms as a guest room, the other I decorated for my niece, Hailey so she could come over whenever and have somewhere to play and sleep.

The men were downstairs showing the delivery men where everything went. My sister and I went to my bedroom and started cutting open boxes to unpack then. When my sister walked in behind me she admired the size of the room.

"Damn girl. This room makes me want to have the layout of my house redone."

"Isn't it crazy big?" I bragged. "I love it so much!"

"I love it, too. I would never come outside if this was my house." Vicky looked around.

"I know, right. I might have to start working from home."

"I can't wait til our house is finished. I'm ready to have my own space."

"You only have a month left. That time will fly by." I told her.

After unpacking almost twenty boxes of clothes and shoes, my sister and I stretched out on my new bed with the plastic still on it. I was so tired of folding clothes. I didn't want to see another item of clothing.

"I'm so proud of you little sister." Vicky was smiling at me. "You might not see it now but getting away from Rick and the drugs business is the best thing for you." She patted my hand.

"I know. I see it already. I can't believe he let me go so easily."

"Maybe he didn't. He might have felt like he owed you your freedom."

"Maybe." I sat up and looked at my sister. "I really want my life to be my top priority. No more putting others before me. I don't want to distance myself from Jay at the same time because he might get hurt and take it the wrong way."

"From what I see, Jay is a good man. Don't let him slip away because you don't know what you want." Vicky advised.

"I know that but I don't want him to think we are something and I end up hurting him."

"You have to work that out right away because he's in love. He about to confess his love for you."

My sister and I gathered some of the boxes and took them downstairs with us. When we got downstairs, Vicky's boyfriend was by himself.

"Where is Jay?"

"Right here."

His hands were full of bags from Boston Market. "Anybody want some chicken?"

"Hell yeah!"

We all stopped what were doing and joined together to eat dinner. After dinner, Vicky and her boyfriend headed out. We hugged and said our goodbyes.

Jay pulled me into his arms. "I finally have you to myself." He kissed my forehead.

"Today has been a crazy day." I put my arms around his head.

"Tell me about it. Please don't move anytime soon."

We were sitting on the couch watching a movie while Jay rubbed my feet. He put my feet on the floor and scooted next to me. He grabbed my hand and started rubbing them.

"I didn't tell you how happy I am for you." He kissed my hand.

"Thank you Jay."

"So now that you are free from Rick, will you give me the pleasure of having you as my lady?"

Jay's eyes where searching mine for an answer. His being so forward surprised me but I knew it was coming soon. Whenever we spent time together, Jay always shared how deeply he felt for me.

"Jay, you know I'm feeling you and all but I just got out of a relationship."

"I understand that. I still feel like our connection is too strong to ignore. Let me show you how it feels to be adored and loved unconditionally."

"I want you too but I need to love myself unconditionally first."

"Okay." He put my hand down. "So where does our friendship go from here?"

"I think I need to take a step back right now."

"What?" He spoke loudly. "This is bullshit." He stood up.

"I'm not saying we can't communicate with each other but I've gotta learn to think for myself. I need to learn what makes me happy before trying to make you happy." I reached out to him. "Now is the time to do this, baby."

"I don't understand. You said you wanted to be with me but now you don't know what you want!"

"I'm sorry Jay."

He stepped away from me and left my new home with hurt feelings in his heart. I didn't know if it was a good idea to let a good man like Jay walk away but I needed to focus on me for once. I wasted so much time trying to mold myself into something Rick could love and want by his side. I didn't want to mold myself for another man. I felt like I had too little time in life to be chasing men. I wanted one to chase me for a change.

~~~~~~~~

For the next few weeks, Jay and I only communicated like twice a week to see how the other was doing. When I heard from him, I wouldn't tell him how much I missed him. I didn't see him at the office anymore. He changed his lunch schedule so he didn't run into me in the lobby. I wanted to see him but I was scared he would reject me.

Those few weeks to myself, I knew Jay was what I wanted. I wanted to make things right between us but he was so distant to me. I gave him a call one day and he forwarded my call to voicemail. I sent him a text message and he responded telling me he was in a meeting. I felt like he was purposely avoiding me. I couldn't blame him. I was the one that wanted some space. I guess I should have been careful of what I wished for.

Rukyyah J. Karreem

Chapter Nineteen
Moni

A month had passed since I told Jay I needed some space. I thought about him a lot and often wondered what it would have been like to be his girl friend. I was really missing Jay but I stopped contacting him. I didn't like when he didn't respond. Rick was facing a court date soon. He was trying to get it postponed but his lawyer hadn't heard back from the court. He called me at least once a week to check up on me. I knew he couldn't walk away from the game. He was still making that money like it was gonna go out of style.

I was on my way back into the office from lunch when I saw Jay and some older lady leaving out for lunch. She had her arm locked around his and they were smiling in each other's face. I was jealous but I tried to be nice by speaking to him.

"Hey Jay. How you been?"

"Things been good Monet. How about you?"

"Great." I looked at the lady. "Can I speak to you for a second?"

"It will have to wait until later. Sondra has taken the time to join me for lunch." She smiled at me like she knew she had what was mine.

"Oh ok. I'll talk to you later." I was steaming hot with jealousy.

"Yeah ok."

Sondra waved to me while Jay held the door open for her. My mind was racing. *Who the fuck was that bitch!* I thought to myself. I was mad at Jay for looking happy with someone else. I wanted to be the lady on his arms. Why wasn't he worried about me? Jay almost looked as if I wasn't there. He wasn't surprised to see me. He didn't look like he missed me.

I went back to my office and kept peeking out the window to see if Jay's car returned to the office. The fifth time I checked, it wasn't out there. I picked up the phone and called his desk phone. I got his voice mail.

I left a message. "Hi Jay. This is Monet. I was seeing if you had a second to talk. Call me later."

I sat at my desk and got through the rest of the day like a zombie. I was hurt over everything that happened over the last few months. I was feeling like everything was coming down on me all at once. I was scared to find out something else negative so I went home and got in my bed at seven p.m. I didn't realize I had dozed off. I was woke out of my sleep by loud knocks on the door. At first I thought I was dreaming but then I jumped up to go answer the door.

When I got to the door, it was Jay standing outside in the rain. I hurried to open the door.

"Why are you standing in the rain? You could have called me to tell me you were outside."

"I tried to give you space Monet." He was upset. "When I saw you today, all my feelings came back and I didn't know what to do with them. I can understand if you still want to be just friends but I wanted to tell you..."

I interrupted him by jumping into his arms and kissing him passionately. Jay wrapped his arms around me and held me like he wasn't ever gonna let me go. He shut the front door behind him and he carried me upstairs to my room.

"I've missed you so much, my beautiful queen." I smiled because in to Jay, I was upgraded to a queen, not a princess.

"I missed you too. I'm so sorry for acting foolishly."

"All has been forgotten."

Jay pushed open my bedroom door with his elbow and carried me to the bed. He slowly took my clothes off and undressed me like he was unwrapping a present. He kissed me all over and touched my body like he had been studying all the things that turned me on. He knew every spot that drove me crazy. He took his time making sure I was comfortable and he was on point with the foreplay.

It had been a long time since I felt sexy like how Jay made me feel. He pressed his full lips against mine and kissed me softly.

"I've waited so long for this moment. I want to remember it for the rest of my life."

"Me too." I kissed him. "I'm so happy you came knocking on my door."

"If you let me, I'll make it my job to make you happy."

"I'd like that." I smiled and then kissed him.

Jay was still fully dressed. I looked him up and down. Then I shook my head. "This isn't gonna work for me honey."

"What." He was confused.

"Take them damn wet clothes off." I smiled.

"Yes ma'am!"

He stood up and did a little strip tease while I admired his whole body. Every aspect of his body was on point. From his sexy smile, his nice muscles, to his lord have mercy size dick. I was very impressed with the full package. Jay rubbed his hand up and down his long shaft making it thicker and longer. After he was completely naked and teased me just a little too much, he lay next to me on my bed. I got on top of Jay and rubbed his muscle-covered chest. I grabbed his strong arms and put them over top his head.

"Don't move them." I demanded.

"What?"

"Don't move your arms. Just trust me."

He put his arms over top his head and held them there for as long as he could. I started licking his body from head to head. I twisted and twirled my tongue in his ear. His arms shook while he tried to make them stay above his head. Then I teased his mouth with my tongue while leaving wet traces over his lips. I softly tongue kissed him. Jay's erect dick was bouncing against my ass while I was sitting on top of him.

"I think he likes me." Referring to his dick.

"I think you're right."

Jay put his hand on my ass and gripped it.

"Oh no baby. I said no moving your arms!"

He put them back over his head then he kissed me. I sucked on his tiny nipples and up and down his six pack stomach. Then I made my way to the second head. I let the muscles in the back of my throat massage the tip of his dick while I moved my head up and down. I came up to the top of his dick and nibbled on it a little bit. I switched back and forth between the two and Jay was losing it. He couldn't keep his arms over his head. He grabbed my leg to slow my motion but I wouldn't stop. His hands were gripping the sheets after I gave him fast tongue strokes to his dick.

"Oh... My... God... Girl!" He spoke loudly.

He did a little jerk before he exploded from the tip of his dick. I thought he would need a minute or two to recuperate from his orgasm but he tapped my leg and motioned to me.

"Come here. Sit it on my face."

He just didn't know what those wonderful words meant to me. I did as Jay demanded and spread myself on top of his face so he could stroke me with his stiff tongue. His tongue darted in and out of me and then he sucked on my clit. He went back and forth. Then he stuck his finger inside me and twirled his tongue around my clit. I dripped my juices down his face and collapsed.

Chapter Twenty
Rick

I wanted to run up on KeKey so bad. I put a price on her. Anybody who ran across her, I needed to know ASAP. I would pay top dollar to kill that bitch! That was real fucked up of her to set me up. All the shit I did for her. I should've known she was a scandalous bitch.

I was sitting outside of Ace's house waiting for him to run me some money he collected for the week. I tried stepping down but when Ace was running shit, the product was moving slow. He wasn't handling business good because he didn't know everything . He wasn't on top of the youngins making sure shit was moving smoothly. He was too nice to them lil' niggas.

I went back to my house where Taneka was waiting for me. She didn't keep my place clean like Moni did. I still didn't trust her yet so I didn't talk to her about the business. She was real immature but she was freaky like I like 'em.

"Did you leave that chicken box on my carpet with all that fucking grease dripping from it?"

"This box is not greasy. It still got chicken in it." She opened the box. "You want some?"

"Hell nah I don't want none of that cold chicken. Get up off my floor and straighten up. I got people coming over in a minute."

"Oh for real? My bad baby. I'll clean up."

I didn't know who taught her to clean. I had to go behind her and clean the living room. Taneka went into my room to change out of her extra large nightshirt and slippers into something presentable. Moni never sat around looking like she was a hot mess. She needed her weave re-done so she put it in a ponytail but you could see the lose tracks at the top. I didn't know what she did with the money I'd given her earlier. She might have given it to her mother.

Before Taneka came out of my room, I sat on the couch and called Moni.

"Hello," she sang into the phone.

"What's up princess?"

"Hey Rick. How are you? Staying out of trouble I hope."

"Yeah. I'm straight shawty. What you been up to?"

"Nothing much. Working and enjoying my new house."

"Oh yeah. You were telling me about it. I was just thinking about you."

"I was thinking about you too. Ain't that funny?"

"What were you thinking?"

117

"I was thinking you might be wildin' out now since you don't have me on your case anymore."

"Whatever!" He laughed. "You know you used to stay on a nigga hard."

"I had to. You don't listen baby."

"I hear you." I heard a little voice laughing in the background. "Who is that?"

"That's my niece. She got me chasing after her."

"Oh okay. I'll hit you up later shawty."

"Okay Rick."

"Still love you girl."

"I know. Love you too."

We hung up and as soon as I turned around Taneka slapped the shit out of me.

"What the fuck was that for?" I yelled.

"Don't be disrespecting me by calling your old bitch on the phone."

"Bitch!" I put my finger in her face. "If you ever put your hands on me again I will choke the shit out you!"

She swung at me and I grabbed her arm. I twisted it and threw her to the floor.

"You lost your fucking mind."

"Why you do that?" She started crying.

"I told you not to play with me."

"You the one on the phone all in love with the ex. You must wanna still be with that bitch."

"Call her out her name one more time and I'ma show you who the bitch is."

"I don't know why you sweating her anyway. She got a man."

"No she don't. Who told you that?"

"My cousin told me. She heard Moni tell her cousin at the hair shop about her new man Jay and she told me about it. She 'on't want cha ass no mor'." She rolled her eyes.

I slapped the taste out her mouth. She grabbed her face and fell to the floor.

"Get your shit and get the fuck out!"

I couldn't stand a smart mouth bitch. I couldn't stand hearing her say Moni was moving on. I didn't think she'd be alone forever but damn, I had no idea. Jay, I thought back. That's the punk ass nigga from her college. I thought I set that nigga straight that he wasn't gon' fuck with what was mine. I was so fucked up. I took a swing at the expensive lamp Moni bought me. When it didn't fall, I picked it up and threw it at the wall. Moni was my princess. She was my heart. I would kill a nigga over her.

Chapter Twenty-One
Moni

It was a little after midnight when I was awakened from my sleep. I was startled because I thought it was an emergency, receiving a call that time of night.

"Hello." I answered while yarning.

"Moni, wake up princess."

"What do you want at this time of night Rick?" I questioned. "Please tell me you aren't locked up again."

"I might as well be. I heard you and that little nigga Jay something serious now."

"We pretty cool."

"Oh yeah. I know you not in love with him. Your heart will always be mine."

"Rick you and I are over. I thought you were letting me go."

"I was giving you time to see what you really wanted. You know it's me baby. Nobody can take care of you like I can."

"Rick, you're right but dirty money don't last always. What's gonna happen when you doing some time? Am I supposed to ask your friends to look after me?"

"You won't have to ask for shit. Plus, I'm not going to jail. I'm above all that shit you yapping about."

"Oh really?"

"Fucking right baby." He laughed. "Don't forget who made it possible for you to live in a big ass house and drive a phat ass ride. Ain't no bitches out there riding like you Moni. That's 'cause I look after what's mine."

"I didn't ask for any of this shit Rick. The money was cool in the beginning but I'd rather you be at home spending quality time with me instead of another chick or chasing money."

"I didn't hear your ass complaining when I was peeling money off for your ass."

"No I wasn't but now I'm being honest with you."

"For real? How about you be honest and come home. Be fucking honest and tell me you still love me. You my princess."

"I will always love you. That's for real but I can't go back to the drama that surrounds you."

Rick was quiet for a second. I didn't know what was going on with him. He seemed a little different. Not as thuggish as he normally was. He almost sound like our breakup softened him a little.

"It sounds like you growing up on me Moni."

"That's what I'm supposed to do baby. I'm still the same Moni I was I just know a little more about a thing or two."

"So would you be too grown to let me come tap that ass real quick?"

"Yes I am Rick! I knew it was something you were calling for."

"Don't play me like that. I'm not making a bootie call. I promise to make it all about you."

"No Rick."

"Come on let me lick that pussy so I can put you back to sleep."

"Good night Rick." I hung up the phone.

I found our conversation to be amusing. I would be lying if I said I was really over Rick. I thought about him all the time. I wondered if he thought about me too. But with Jay, it was so much more. He showed me how to really love. He taught me how to really appreciate life. Everyday, he was the first thought on my mind. He was what got me through a bad day.

I rolled over in my bed and started thinking about both the relationships I had. I was thankful to receive so much money and presents from Rick. Without him, I would still be living in my mother's public housing. He was the one who put up the money to help my mother move into a house of her own. I didn't miss those days living in public housing. My friends always teased me because I always had my sister's hand-me downs. I thought my family was pretty wealthy until a little girl from school teased me about my mother picking me and my sister up from school on the city bus one day. She had a PTA meeting for both of us. My mother always made ends meet so I didn't think there was a problem with the way we lived.

I rolled over with the thoughts of Jay and Rick. My thoughts quickly changed from reminiscing about the good times we shared to the amazing sex I had with them. Rick was my first sexual partner and lover so he was very memorable. He was much rougher than Jay but they both satisfied me differently. Jay was the hopeless romantic who swept me off my feet every moment he got. He wrote me erotic poetry and emailed them to me. When I read them at work, I would start grinding slowly in my seat just to relieve the stiffness of my clit. Jay sent me all types of flowers. For each assortment, he had a beautiful poem that made me feel extra beautiful. He cooked for me. He would massage me without having to ask. He made me crave him physically and mentally. I really did want to have him in my life forever.

Rick was the type that wanted to fuck me anywhere. He handled his business by bending me over in his car, fucking me against the wall, anything rough he enjoyed it. So did I. He tried to tap into his romantic side a few times but he wasn't natural with it. I wouldn't be surprised if he ran his ideas by a friend to find out what I would enjoy. He thought money was what I really wanted and all along I wanted him.

It didn't stop my body from aching to feel the touch of a man. I wanted my body to be caressed and licked from head to toe. My hands took over as they listened to what my body wanted. I rubbed my nipples until they rose and stood hard. I traced my nipples with little circles and then parted my legs to give myself some love.

I spread my lips with my fingers and found my treasure. I played with my clit like it was my favorite toy. I moaned softly from the excitement I gave myself. The sound of my wetness made me more excited. Then in my mind, Jay took over. He licked my shaved pussy inside out. He spread my legs and then wrapped them around his head. I suffocated him while he kept his tongue stiff and strong. He kept twirling his tongue and then softly sucking on my lips between my legs. He stuck his tongue inside me and fucked me until I came.

Of course I wasn't finished. *Turn that ass over*, Rick told me in my mind. I rolled over and positioned myself to ride him. I burred my face into my pillows then started rotating my hips and grinding like I was working a dick. I felt Rick's hand grip my hips holding me right were he needed me to be. He slapped my ass hard and then rubbed it like he was wishing on the lucky tree on *Showtime at the Apollo*. I reached my fingers between my legs until I found the dripping wet opening. I stuck my fingers in and rode them. My fingers were dripping wet. I felt the wetness drip down to the palm of my hand and down my thigh.

After I came, I reached into my naughty drawer next to my bed and pulled out my nine inch black vibrator and my bullet. I powered the bullet and stuck it in me. The vibration was so powerful it stimulated my ass hole too. I ran my finger over the tingling sensation and released a loud moan. *You like that shit?*

"Yes baby. That shit is nice." I moaned.

Back that ass up on this dick, Rick demanded.

"Okay, daddy! Like this?" I moaned.

Don't forget about me. Jay whispered as he sat at top of my bed and leaned against the headboard.

"You know I can't forget about you baby."

I pulled the vibrator closer to me as I licked and sucked it like it really was Jay.

I came once more after picturing Jay and Rick pleasing me like they did at the same time. My naughty fantasy was put to work while making love to myself. I enjoyed the shock my body was in after coming so much. I felt like I had a dirty secret just between me, myself, and I.

Chapter Twenty-Two
Moni

I pretty much was floating after my night. I slept so good that I didn't bother hitting the snooze button. I jumped out of bed and was ready to face the world. I took a fifteen-minute shower and then I walked around my house naked just for the hell of it.

I was smiling ear to ear when I got to my job. I opened the door to my office and the lights were already on. At first I thought the cleaning crew left it on after cleaning it the night before but I couldn't miss the big, white box with a red ribbon on my desk. I started laughing and then walked over to my desk to see what was inside. I opened it and found a little black teddy bear holding a framed picture of Jay and I that we took with his digital camera. There was also a card inside. I picked it up to read it and realized it was a scavenger hunt clue. After putting my ideas together, I realized the next clue was under my keyboard. I picked it up and grabbed the next clue, which lead me to underneath my desk. When I pulled my chair out, there was another clue that lead me to the back of my office door. I went to the door and there was Jay standing stiff and about to burst into laughter.

"Oh my God, Jay! What are you doing?" I was startled.

"I wanted to see how good you were at this game." He laughed so hard.

His face was bright red from laughing so hard. He had to get himself together from cracking up before he could speak. After he got himself together he pulled me close to him.

"So what did you think you would find?"

"I don't know. I didn't think it would be you." I kissed him.

"It was hard as hell to keep myself from laughing." He smiled.

"I'm glad you had your morning laugh at my expense." I hit him playfully.

"It was great!" He hugged me. "It was funny hearing you searching and searching."

"You think you slick don't you?"

"A little bit. So how about you close your eyes real quick."

"Why?"

"Just do it!"

I closed my eyes and I heard Jay open something. I tried peak but he moved away from in front of me. Shortly after, he came up behind me and placed a necklace around my neck.

"Okay. You can open them now." He told me.

I opened my eyes and looked down at the necklace. It was a beautiful past, present, and future white gold necklace with three diamonds.

The diamonds were at least two carats with a circle cut. I couldn't take my eyes off how lovely it looked on my chest. I turned around and jumped into Jay's arms.

"I love it! I love it!"

"Really? 'Cause I love you too."

"Love you too!" I hugged him tightly around his head and the kisses him softly. He set me down on the top of my desk and kissed me passionately.

"I'ma tear your ass up when we get off from work!"

"Why you can't do it now?" I teased by widely opening my legs.

"Don't play with me. You know I'm young and my dick get hard when the wind blows."

"Lemme see." I put my hands down his pants.

"Oh yeah. He's definitely at attention."

"That's what you do to it." He smiled with a naughty grin.

I gave him a hand job. I didn't take my eyes off his eyes and we kissed like we were gonna fuck. I was aching for him to stick it in me but I knew others would start arriving in the office soon. I didn't want the office smelling like sex so I continued squeezing and pulling his dick until it was doubled in sized and he came. The look in his eyes was pure satisfaction. His knees buckled and leaned over me to regain his composure.

Chapter Twenty-Three
KeKey

It was going on six o'clock when I was getting ready for my date with Trent. I was so happy he talked me into moving to Philly with him. I needed to lay low for a little bit. We had gotten so close before I moved to Philly. For the first time, I thought I might actually be falling in love. Besides Trent being super sexy, he was a very good listener. We talked for hours at a time about my childhood and my lift I left in Maryland.

Trent really was cool because he let me stay at his condo that he was thinking about renting out to tenants. The condo was in Old City Philadelphia. The whole condo was bigger than some houses I'd seen in Maryland. The living room was very spacious with expensive white leather furniture accented with plants and art pieces. The kitchen was huge. The entire kitchen had black appliances. The island in the kitchen had a hunter green marble top on it with beautiful black bar stools sitting around it. The bedrooms were equally beautiful and the bathroom was exceptional. It was as big as a bedroom with a huge tub in the center. There was a stand in shower in the far right corner with a crystal clean glass door.

The area was really beautiful like downtown Annapolis. The buildings had that same historic look. The sidewalk had bright red bricks just like my hometown. It made me home sick. Old City sometimes made me feel like I was a hood girl out of place. There were nice museums and restaurants. Everywhere Trent and I went, I felt classy. I must admit, I really looked good on his arm.

Trent met me at the condo. He was looking good in his blue Polo shirt and khaki pants. Trent was that sexy sophisticated thug you could dress up and take him out for a night on the town. You can dress him down in some hood wear and hang tight with him too.

When Trent arrived, I was still dressing. He looked around and admired the way I kept his place cleaned. I had no reason not to keep it looking good. He let me stay there rent free. He walked into the kitchen to grab a drink from the refrigerator. After pouring himself a glass of orange juice, he sat down at the island and gulped it down.

"You really got it smelling good up in here." He walked over to the sink and put his empty glass in it. "Is that a candle?"

I joined him in the kitchen after putting my hair in a side bun. He was sitting at the island talking loudly so I could still hear him from a distance. Once he realized I walked in the kitchen, he pulled a stool out so I could sit across from him.

"No. My sister buys those from bath and works. It's one of those wall plug-in thingy." I thought back to how I missed my sister, Steph. "She must have given me a thousand of them when I was home. I think I brought all of them with me."

"So does any of your family know you're up here in Philly?" he questioned with curiosity all over his face.

"No. I didn't tell anybody. That would be too risky. I didn't want them telling anybody were I was. Every time I call, I still block the number."

"Seriously! That's crazy," he insisted. "That's your family. I'm sure you can trust them."

"I can trust my sister but I don't want her to get involved."

"Do she know how deep you got involved with the game?"

"What do you mean?" I asked offensively.

"Do she know you knocked a man off?" He raised an eyebrow.

"No. She doesn't know about anything. She could care less about where all my money came from. I told her I worked niggas for their paper and that's the story I'm sticking too."

"Okay, baby. I'm not trying be all in your business." He laughed. "You about to snap my neck." I started laughing with him. "By the way, did I tell you how sexy you look in that dress?"

Trent looked me up in down while his eyes searched my body. He leaned forward and put his elbows on the top of the island.

"No you didn't." I smiled.

I loved being complimented by a super sexy man. It made me feel good all over. It made my body tingle from head to toe. I was feeling like a beautiful woman with Trent. Not the hood bitch everyone known me as in Annapolis.

"You look good enough to eat." He licked his lips.

"Really, baby." I blushed. "How about you eat me and tell me do I taste the same way I look."

"Baby you know I'll make them cute little toes of yours wiggle and make your eyes cross," he bragged. Trent jumped up from his stool and pushed it back when he moved. He lifted me up off the stool and sat me on the island. "Spread them legs so daddy can taste that pretty pussy of yours."

I did as he wished. I spread my legs and lay back on the island like I was a turkey about to get stuffed for Thanksgiving dinner. I was dripping on the island from the anticipation of him eating me. Trent didn't disappoint me at all. He sucked and licked my clit like it was his last meal. My body was shaking and trembling while I enjoyed the rush he sent threw my body. Trent wasn't coming up for air. He licked me until I came.

~~~~~~~~

Trent and I arrived at the Brasil's Restaurant on Chestnut Street. We decided to eat from the buffet were there was an assortment of with

Brazilian food. We stuffed our faces. I ate so much food my stomach looked like I was four months pregnant. Good thing my bright pink dress wasn't form fitting. Afterwards, we enjoyed the South American style music they had playing. We sat at our table enjoying the music and letting our full bellies go down a little.

"That food was off the hook wasn't it?" Trent asked while leaning back in his seat to get a little more comfortable.

"Hell yeah," I agreed. "That was on point. I'm happy you brought me to this spot. It might be my new favorite place to eat while I'm in Philly." I smiled.

"I hope you plan on making this a permanent place to stay." Trent grabbed my hand and rubbed it. "I'm really starting to feel for you, Ms. Keyshawn Hoyt."

"Nigga, don't be calling me out my government name." I laughed. "This damn table could be tapped."

Trent eyes widened and looked around. He scooted his chair close to mine.

"Damn, baby. If this table tapped, we might both go to jail tonight if they knew how we really handle business."

"I definitely don't want see you sitting in jail as fine as you look." I leaned over and kissed him.

"Really?" He smiled. "I would be able to handle myself though. Ain't no nigga smart enough to try test me. They know me up and down the streets of Philly, DC, Baltimore and

Annapolis. You name it, baby. I handle my business all over," he said with confidence.

"I feel you, baby." I leaned close to him and spoke lower. "At one point of my life I wanted to be a bad ass bitch and run shit from state to state but the shit that went down with Tiny and my mom, it had me shook for real. I still have nightmares about somebody coming after me to kill me," I said sadly.

"You don't have to worry about shit up here, baby. Don't nobody know you here or know who you are." He looked me in my eyes and made me want a repeat session of what we did in the kitchen. "When you with me, baby, you never have to worry.

Trent looked at me with sincerity all over his face. He was really falling for me and I felt it. He made me feel safe with him. He definitely had my back.

We leaned in and kissed each other. Our lips were connected and I was lost in Trent like we were the only people in the restaurant. I was with him and he made it known every second he got that I was important to him. He always wanted me to know he didn't want me to leave. He wanted me to stay in Philly because he was falling hard for me.

Chapter Twenty-Four
Moni

I felt the covers being pulled off my face and then the sun greeted me. I tried to adjust my eyes but the light was too bright. I pulled the covers back over my face for it to be pulled back down again. I yanked the covers back but they wouldn't move. I let the cover go and Jay pulled it all the way off me. He exposed my naked body.

"Rise and shine my beautiful queen. " He greeted me with a smile.

His smile was a great start to any day. He was excited to wake up next to me. He was staring down at me like how a father does his sleeping baby. I smiled back at him.

"Good morning my sexy king," I said in my sleepy voice. "It's good waking up to you this morning." I started sniffing around because the aroma of bacon and French toast was strong. "You cooked breakfast?"

"Yes I did."

He moved out of the way to show me the tray of food sitting on the nightstand. I sat up in the bed and wondered what the occasion was. Not only did Jay have plates filled with French toast, bacon, eggs and sliced strawberries, he had a little vase with a long stem rose and an envelope.

"Baby, what is all this for?"

My eyes were searching his. I waited for his response. He always had something slick up his sleeves. Jay got a big kick out of watching me be blissful when he gave me gifts or surprises.

"It's for you."

Jay walked over to the food and brought it back to the bed. He ate a slice of the bacon on his way over. He smiled at how good it tasted.

"Did you think I had your birthday mixed up?" He looked at me like he wouldn't dare forget such an important date for me. "I have my calendar marked, baby. I wouldn't let it slip my mind."

"I thought you wouldn't but since it is a few days before, I thought you were mistaken." Jay moved the tray out his way then he grabbed my leg and pulled me close to him. "Boy! What the hell you doing?"

Jay took my big toe and sucked on it. He put the whole thing in his mouth. I watched as my bright orange colored toenail disappeared in and out of his mouth.

"You know you like it, Monet," He said in his very deep sexy voice.

Jay licked all my toes and massaged my feet. He might as well have been playing with my pussy because it was dripping wet. He kept sucking until I was shaking my leg trying to get him to let it go.

"Baby! Oh... my... please stop," I moaned loudly.

"Sorry, I didn't understand you," he teased.

He grabbed my ankles and started nibbling on them one at a time.

"You know you gotta fuck me now," I stated.

Jay put my legs down as he dropped his boxer exposing his well hung dick. He rubbed it and then tapped it against my leg.

"Is this what you want baby?"

He was standing there, looking damn fine holding his dick in his hand. The more he touched it, the more it grew. The more it grew, the more I wanted it in mouth and in my pussy. Jay climbed on top of me into a sixty-nine position. He looked even bigger from that angle. It was a little awkward at first but once I got used to sucking him while lying on my back, there was no turning back. I felt like Jay was doing pushups the way he was going down licking the cat and then pumping his dick in and out of my mouth.

My skills were so on point that I made Jay come in five minutes. He still was working on me after he got his nut. He lay down next to me, rolled me over and pulled me on top of his face. I rode his tongue for five more minutes before I squirted and my juices flowed down his chin.

After our morning freak'em session, Jay and I fell asleep. I woke up before Jay did. He was slightly snoring. Listening to him snore almost sounded therapeutic for me. It was slightly above a whisper but not loud enough for me to kick him on the floor. I sat up in the bed and looked at the tray of food. Our food was cold and untouched. I had forgotten all about the envelope so I slipped out of the bed and walked over to the tray to pick it up. The envelope was sealed with a shiny gold sticker that read, *here is my heart*, in a heart shape.

I broke the seal by pulling the opening hard. Inside the envelope was a piece of light pink paper that was scented. I pulled it out and read it. It read:

> *Jonathon Jackson*
> *Loves*
> *Monet Harrison*

It was written in calligraphy. My eyes lit up in excitement. My heart felt like I was experiencing what love really was. Just to think I was gonna let this good man just walk out of my life because I didn't know what I wanted.

I jumped on the bed and woke Jay out of his sleep.

"Baby, wake up! Wake up, baby!" I was jumping up in down. "This is soooo cute!" I waved the paper in his face. "I can't believe how sweet you are to me. And what is this scent? I love it, too!"

Jay was looking at me like I had lost my damn mind. I was yapping on and on and he was trying to get his rest on. He looked at the paper and he sat up.

"Girl, where you get all that damn energy from?" He grabbed me by the waist and pulled me down. "Come on back to bed." He cuddled me into his arms.

"Baby, did you hear me? I love the paper with our names on it!" I kissed him. "You are so thoughtful."

He put my hand on his chest and he rubbed it. He looked me in my eyes then smiled.

"Yeah, baby. It would have been nice if we had the same last names."

He searched my face for a response.

I didn't know what to say. I was astonished. I loved Jay but wasn't ready to make a lifetime commitment with him. I still had feelings I was trying to suppress for Rick. I knew I couldn't commit to another man with him still holding a place in my heart. I didn't want to seem like I didn't care so I brushed those thoughts aside.

"Would that mean you'd take my last name?" I joked.

"Of course not. That's so gay." Jay kissed me on my forehead and held me tighter. I put my head on his chest and listened to his heart beat. I felt like Jay was doing a good job at making me happy. I hoped he felt the same way about me. I was really new to the grown-up relationship but I was getting pretty used to feeling beautiful all the time.

Chapter Twenty-Five
KeKey

I woke up to Trent sitting on the lounge chair he had in the bedroom. He was sitting there keying a message into his Black Berry. He looked like he was trying to be quiet. When his eyes caught mine, he was startled.

"Damn, baby. I didn't know you woke up," He said while putting his Black Berry in his pocket. "You don't even stretch or yarn when you get up. No movement at all."

"I don't. All that stuff is unnecessary." I set up with the cover over my bare breast. "Plus, you never know who you gotta sneak up on when you awake. You don't wanna alert everyone about your every move."

He laughed and looked at me like I was crazy. "What you talking about? Why would you have to sneak up on somebody after you wake up?"

I looked at him wondering why he didn't understand. You never knew what was going on when you did dirty shit. Everyday I woke up I was surprised someone didn't try kill me in my sleep.

"What if somebody drugged you and had your ass sitting in a cold basement waiting for that ass to wake up. They walking around, killing time, 'cause they need some information you hiding. Do you want them to know you woke up or will you just try to fucking bounce?"

He laughed.

"I guess I never thought about anything like that. I love the way your mind work."

"Yeah see, you thought I was just talking out my head didn't you?"

"Naw, baby. I knew you were gonna put me down. You always think like a man." He smiled.

"Yes I do. So you gon' tell me who you sending a message to from your Black Berry this time of morning?" I looked over at the clock on the nightstand. "'Cause you damn sure stopped when you saw I was up. Did I interrupt you little message?" I looked at him like I was ready for any bullshit he was about to lay on me.

He thought about a good response while he was staring at me. He leaned back in the chair and intertwined his fingers.

"Baby. I don't have shit to hide from you. I told you. You can trust me."

"Really? Well lemme see your phone."

"What the fuck? Are you serious, baby?"

"Fucking right. Bring me the damn phone."

I was steaming hot. He was acting like he had shit he was covering up. I don't like the role of being the dumb bitch. That wasn't me. I refused to be another Moni and Rick. I got off the bed and walked up to Trent, who didn't flinch at all. I went in his pocket and retrieved the phone. I searched his saved and sent messages. There was nothing there. I stared him in the eyes because I was confused.

"Wondering why there are no text messages?" he questioned.

"Yeah. What, you deleted them?"

I rolled my eyes and crossed my bare breast.

"No but check the calendar." He smiled devilishly.

I went through his calendar and I was so surprised. Trent stored in a message for today. It read:

Call the jewelry store we walked past to order those diamond earrings.

I looked at Trent to see if the message was real. We were out shopping the night before and we walked past Bernie Robbins. I couldn't help but to do a double take when I walked past all the sparkling diamonds.

"Oh damn, them things blinking right there." I pointed to the diamond earrings that looked too heavy to wear in your ears. "Look at them right there." I showed Trent another pair. Then I laid eyes on some really fly ass earrings. They were dangly white gold earrings that had four diamonds in a horizontal row and then there was a large diamond shape diamond that was filled with diamonds surrounded by yellow gold. It was love at first sight. "Awe, baby, them things are right! I love those. We gotta go see them up close." I told Trent.

We walked inside the store and admired them up close. They were even more beautiful than from the window.

"They are the shit," Trent said. "Damn, they high as shit though." He looked as if they lost their beauty after he saw the price on them.

"Not for you big money grip. I see the ride you got. You flip homes just as much as you flip coke so I know you got paper."

"Baby, you still have to put money into them homes first before selling and renting. Nobody gon' buy a busted ass house." He got closer to me. "Plus, I don't know what coke you talking 'bout." He winked his eye at me.

"Okay baby," I whispered.

~~~~~~~~

I was getting tired of sitting outside the abandoned building, which looked like it was once a 7-Eleven. Trent was supposed to be meeting up with this dude from New York for some pure cocaine. He was supposed to be there at midnight but it was going on 12:30. Trent was getting irritated but he didn't speak on it. He sat in the back seat looking cooler than a mafucka.

When the nigga finally pulled up in his Jag forty minutes late, I was pissed off.

"You need to keep some of your money for a reimbursement or some shit for the time we sat

143

here looking like asses," I stipulated. "This shit is foul business."

"Baby, calm down." Trent grabbed my hands to calm me. "Some shit is unexpected. We have to deal wit' it and keep it moving." He looked at me to see if I was calm. "Are you gonna take care of this for me?" He handed me a duffle bag.

"Yeah I got this for you, baby." I grabbed the bag and then opened my door. I turned to Trent and kissed him. "Be right back, sexy. Don't leave me." I laughed.

"I'd be a fool to leave something as fine as you." He tapped my ass while I got out the car.

"I like that shit!" I laughed.

I walked up to the Jag and tapped on the window. I stood there for a second and no one stepped out or rolled the window down. I tapped one more time then I was gonna run my ass back to the car just in case some niggas were trying set my ass up. Before I could get my finger on the window, it started rolling down.

"What a beautiful lady like you doing handing a grown man's business?"

He smiled, showing off his platinum grill in his mouth.

My eyes lit up with fear. Those were the same words Tiny's crew used when they were trying to kill me. I dropped the duffle bag to my feet and I was frozen. I couldn't move to pick it up. I felt like my soul jumped out of my body and I was watching a bad movie starring me.

The tall, athletic built, caramel complexion pretty boy opened the car door and stepped out. He bent down to my feet and picked up the duffle bag.

"Pretty lady, you can't be dropping this type of paper on the ground and shit. Somebody can do anything to you and bounce with the paper and the coke." He looked at me to see if I was paying attention. I was unresponsive. "Baby girl, did you hear me?"

"Oh I'm sorry. Yeah. Good looking out." I grabbed the big ass bag from his hand and ran to the car like my life depended on it. I was so shook I felt like I was about to shit myself.

"You ok?" Trent asked. "You're not looking too right, babe." He was looking me up and down. I sat down next to him and then he pulled me into his arms. "What happened out there? You look like you saw a fucking ghost or something."

"I'm ok. I must have gotten dizzy," I lied. "But I'm straight."

"Okay 'cause I wanna run some business by you." He smiled with his sexy grin.

"Do share baby."

"How about we take a little trip to Annapolis this weekend?"

"Hell no!" I yelled. "I'm not going back there. I will be leaving in a body bag."

"You're paranoid. I'm not gonna let shit happen to you. I need to make a trip down Annapolis. Some niggas that run with Rick want some coke from me."

"Word? Them niggas pay top dollar too, baby."

"I know this. That's why I want you to go with me. Them niggas like your family."

"They more like ex boyfriends. You wish they would disappear." I laughed.

"Oh shit. Why you feel like that, baby?"

"Let's just say I don't trust them and they for damn sure don't trust me."

Going back to Annapolis was the last thing on my mind. I cared for Trent a lot but I wasn't trying to sacrifice my life for him. He was asking too much. He could have easily gone to Annapolis without me. Now it seemed like the closer we got, the more he involved me in his shit. Just like Rick.

Chapter Twenty-Six
Moni

It was midnight on May 4, 2007, my twenty-first birthday. Jay and I still were wide-awake because we took the day off to celebrate. We were in the living room drinking a bottle of wine and watching my favorite DVD, *ATL*. We were curled up on the couch with a big bowl of buttered popcorn and a cozy blanket. We were cracking up off the movie like it was our first times seeing it.

Jay pulled the blanket off himself and then reached for the remote that was on the coffee table. He paused the movie and then stood to his feet.

"Baby, you want anything while I'm up?" He asked while smiling at me.

"No baby. Where you going?"

I looked at him like he was tripping pausing my movie. My favorite part of the movie was just about to play. Jay looked at me like he knew he was wrong. He disappeared for a little bit and I was tempted to let the movie play.

I heard some rumbling going on in my coat closet then I grew inquisitive of what Jay was doing. It sounded like he must have hurt himself on something because there were loud commotions.

"Fuck!" he yelled.

"Are you ok baby?"

I was worried.

"Yeah babe. I'm good."

Jay came out of the closet rubbing the side of his head and he was carrying a gift box.

"I thought you said you would give me my gift later."

"I will but I wanted to get this out of the way." He handed me the box while grabbing the bowl of popcorn. "Here. Open it."

The box was kind of heavy. He sat anxiously while I opened the gift.

I started laughing when I opened the gift. I hit Jay playfully on his arm. "What in the world is this for?" I asked while holding a bottle of sun block.

"Keep going." He smiled. "It's more in there." He pointed to the box.

I moved the stuffing paper around and then I found a can of shaving cream.

"What you trying say, Jay? You think I need a shave?"

I rolled my eyes at him and then smiled.

"No baby." He laughed and then pointed to the box. "Keep going." The last gift I pulled from the box was a sexy little black bikini. His was smiling at the bikini like he enjoyed the gift a little too much. "Do you like it?"

"Of course I do. I guess I need to get right to wear my bikini right?" I laughed. "Where we going, Sandy Point or Ocean City?" I was excited about the idea of getting my swim on at the beach.

"Neither, baby. Just know we will be on the beach on Saturday."

"Okay, baby. I'ma have to go 'head hook up my legs and bikini line before I hit the beach. Is that cool with you?"

"Do what you like, baby." He kissed my forehead. "We gonna have so much fun for your birthday weekend."

Jay was looking at me like he was holding the best secret ever. He got back under the covers and un-paused the movie. He reached on the table to get the bowl of popcorn while I rubbed his back. I knew my birthday was gonna be a good one to remember.

Chapter Twenty-Seven
Moni

There was a knock at my door a little after two pm. I was in my bedroom so the doorbell was ringing off the hook. I thought it was Jay because he went home to finish packing and he was gonna pick up a few things he needed for our weekend trip. I was wondering why he didn't use his extra key.

"I'm coming!" I yelled so he could stop ringing the damn door.

"Happy Birthday princess," Rick said with a little thuggish grin that made me melt.

What the hell was he doing at my door? I didn't know if I was mad at him or excited to see him. He was standing there looking good in his top dollar casual clothes. He was looking so damn fine. He gave the very sexy Stringer Bell from the Wire a run for his money. I was trying to control the instant wetness I developed between my legs but I couldn't. Why did he have to show up looking like that? I was staring at him like I wanted to jump on him at the front door.

"Um... Thank you, Rick," I finally got my thoughts together. "What are you doing here?"

"You know I couldn't stay away on my beautiful princess birthday," He smiled. "You only turn twenty one once." He turned around and admired my patio and the rest of the outside of my house. "I'm glad my money did some good for you, baby."

I often thought the same thing. Rick was very generous when it came to his money and me. Whatever I wanted, I got. Rick spoiled me with his paper. He never cared about price tags when he knew he fucked up with me or making sure I was happy with him. I never doubted his love for me but I knew I deserved better. I was telling myself those exact words until I heard words slip out of my mouth.

"Would you like to come in?"

I felt nervous having him in my house.

"Yeah. But I have to get something for you."

He walked over to my small bushes and pulled out a lot of large gift bags. I wanted to jump up in down when I saw the bags. I knew it would be something hot. I opened the bags and found three pair of Baby Phat Jeans with shirts to match. There were two coach handbags with matching wallets. There was a small box with five carat platinum diamond earrings. They were beautiful. I jumped into his arms.

"You are too much, Rick," I told him as he hugged me tight. "Thank you so much." I kissed him.

We gazed into each other's eyes and Rick started kissing me with a lot of passion. I didn't stop him. I didn't want him to stop. He carried me into my house and shut the door behind him while he still was kissing and holding me. Rick ripped off my Vote Obama t-shirt and exposed my half naked body. He then ripped my pink laced boy shorts, which left me naked.

Rick and I were bumping into everything on our way into the living room. We didn't make it to the couch. Rick put me down and started pulling at his belt while I unbuttoned his shirt. His shoes and belt went flying and I jumped on top of him. He caressed my ass while I was in his arms. He sucked my nipples so hard, I thought he was gonna leave a passion mark. Rick let me slide out of his arms and he licked my body while loud moans released from my mouth. Rick had a mouthful of my breast in his mouth when he started fingering me. His dick was hard as an aluminum bat when it tapped up against my thigh.

Rick folded my legs as far as they could go into my chest and then he dug deep into my pulsating wetness. He went so deep I thought he was trying to feel my stomach from between my legs. Rick was moaning loud with each stroke. He was working the pussy slow then he would speed it up.

"Tell me it's still mine Moni," he moaned.

"It's still your, Rick," I moaned.

He made the strangest face and then he came. He collapsed on top of me and then kissed me.

"Damn I almost forgot how good it was."
He smiled.

"No, baby. You'll never forget that," I
teased.

As Rick took me into his arms, the reality of
what we did came to me. I was scared and
didn't know if I should kick Rick out or let him
hold me. I didn't want him to leave but I didn't
want him to feel like sex was something we could
share whenever he wanted it.

"Oh my God, Rick! You have to go." I
panicked. "You have to go now. Jay is on his
way back here shortly."

"You know I'm not scared of that nigga."
He smiled rubbing his dick.

"Rick, he is my boyfriend. You have to go.
Please. Just do it for me."

Before Rick could respond, my cell phone
started ringing. My heart jumped in my stomach
when I heard Jay's ringtone. I put my finger to
my mouth to tell Rick to be quiet. He looked at
me like he could do whatever he wanted to.

"Hey baby," I answered, faking being
chipper.

"You need anything from the store? I have
to pick up some toothpaste."

"Yes." I felt like a ton of bricks lifted off me.
"Can you get me some body wash, feminine
wipes and some chocolate?" I knew he would
need some time to decide where to find those
items.

"Damn, girl. Okay. I'll see you soon." He
hung up.

Rick still was in the floor naked like he didn't hear me. I looked at him like I was gonna get him out of my house. Finally he got up and got dressed.

"You still my love princess." He kissed me. "I won't fuck with cha happiness though."

He grabbed his stuff and got out before Jay came back. I was straightening up so that nothing looked out of place. I hid all my gifts deep in the back of my clothes and then I ran back down stairs. When I got to the last step, Jay unlocked the door and walked in. I jumped like I saw a ghost.

"Hey baby, I'm back," he announced.

He was excited to see me. I was smiling like I couldn't wait for him to get back. Then I almost fell on my face when I realized my ripped panties were underneath the coffee table.

Chapter Twenty-Seven
Rick

It was fucked up to see my girl more concerned for her new nigga like I wasn't shit. I knew she still loved me but she didn't wanna tell that bitch ass nigga Jay. He got one chance to fuck Moni over and I'ma put the barrel of my gun to his temple.

Even though I could have any chick I wanted, it was nothing like the connection I shared with Moni. I liked how she held onto my shoulders like she didn't wanna let me go while I was in her. Her kisses were soft and they made me feel good. I wanted to give her the world if I could. She used to be down for everything but she must've gotten tired of my shit. If she had held on a little longer, she definitely would have been my wifey.

After I got home and washed the sex off of me, I sat on the side of my bed with my towel wrapped around my waist. Moni decided to keep it moving. On top of the shit that happened in Philly, I spent a lot of time re-evaluating my life.

155

I knew I needed to make some changes fast but I couldn't give up all the money. I loved not having to worry about when my next payday was coming. I pretty much got paid on a daily basis. Sometimes I got paid a hell of a lot more, depending on if I was pushing coke to my little street crew or selling brief cases of coke to niggas tryina flip that shit to make them real dollars.

Every night, it was getting harder and harder for me to fall asleep. My mind was always gone on some shit I did to fuck up people's lives. I was feeding the addiction of pretty much all the local addicts. It didn't matter if they sniffed, shot up, or smoked it out of a glass dick, I was their suppliers.

I was the reason crack heads let a nigga fuck their young daughter just for a hit. If they were really hard up, they would let a whole group of niggas get at her child. I've seen people steal from their mommas to buy a hit. I've taken people's last dollar to make my stash fatter. I've broken up families. I have taken a man from his wife and children because he couldn't walk away from his habit.

The shit was laying heavy on my brain. I walked into my kitchen and poured a double shot of Hennessey on the rocks. I went in the hidden drawer of my bar and then pulled out my stash of weed. I sat at the bar while I rolled up a blunt. I smoked it and drank my drink like I was washing my thoughts away. Half way through the blunt, I wasn't feeling a buzz so I poured myself another double shot. After finishing my drink and the whole blunt, I was feeling like none of my thoughts or issues mattered.

Who gave a fuck that people got fucked up on my product? My shit was what was poppin'in Maryland. I had dope boys all over. I had them in small and big cities. Slinging drugs to bring me back a wealthy profit. I wasn't greedy either. I let them little niggas keep a lot of my money for the hard work they did. If they were wise, they would save up some of that money to make their own distribution or start a business that was funded by drug money. If they were a clown ass nigga, they spent their money and had nothing to show for it but some fresh shoes, couple clothes, and a chicken head that thought she was a dime.

I started hustling when I was sixteen. For the first year, I hustled after school for a street level nigga name Taz. I thought that nigga had money out the ass. He had a nice new ride and always kept a different chick with him. He stayed fresh with new gear, too. I was with him all the time. If he had a job that needed to be handled, I did it. One day I was on top of the hill down 20 running to all the sells before them other niggas could beat me to it. Out of no where, this nigga rolled up on me in his car. He rolled down his dark tinted window and he smiled at me a little bit.

"Hey little nigga!" He pointed to me. I pointed to my chest questioning who he was talking to. "Yeah you. Co' mere."

I was a little scared at first because I never seen the nigga before in my life. He was looking at me like he didn't wanna harm me but you never know.

"What you want from me? You don't look like you buying," I stated wisely.

He laughed and cocked his eyes to the side then the back door was pushed open from the inside.

"Your name Rick, right?" He asked. I shook my head to agree. "I see you out here handling your business for that small timer, Taz."

"Yeah we getting this paper. You feel me?" I grinned.

"Nonsense, little man." I got my promotion from little nigga. "You need to be making real money. Are you ready for a grown man's business?"

My eyes lit up with dollar signs. I thought the five hundred a week I was making with Taz was real money but the man was telling me I'd make three times that amount if I made a switch. I got in the car with him. He introduced himself as Franklin. I soon found out he was the real big time nigga back in my younger days. Franklin was one of Tiny's niggas. He was the closest to him so he made sure he made top dollar. The first thing he did was hook me up with my first blunt and my first threesome. I had two young girls about five years older than me. They both took turns sucking and fucking every inch of me. From that day forth, it was no stopping me. I had to have the money and bitches.

Chapter Twenty-Eight
KeKey

It took a lot of convincing from Trent to pick up the phone to call Moni to wish her a happy birthday. It wasn't that I didn't want to speak to her but I was worried that she wouldn't wanna talk to me once she knew it was me. I did a lot of fucked up shit in our friendship and all she had done was treat me like a sister.

Maybe there was a tiny bit of jealousy of Moni. Everything was always handed to her and I had to work hard, steal, or fuck for what I wanted. It was no shame in my game. Like they all say, *you gotta use what you got to get what you want.* I used to live by those words to the fullest.

Moni grew up in the same neighborhood. Once my father died, my mother was forced to sell our house and she moved into public housing. My father, Randy, was a local drug dealer who turned into a crack addict. He was well known on the streets even after he turned into a user, a lot of people showed respect for him and looked after his family. My father started selling my mother's jewelry and then appliances from the house for a hit. He was once was a thick, tall man about 6'1. After his habit took over, he was about 150 pounds. His face lost its fullness and his bright smile turned into different shades of yellow and brown.

I started hating my father because younger people knew him as a crack head and everybody knew he was my father. I would hear stories of him robbing the old 7-Eleven that was on Forest Drive across the street from Safeway, which came many years later. My mother still loved him but she didn't like who he turned into. When he came home, he slept in the basement and wasn't allowed upstairs until after we left the house. It was summer of '91 when my father died from an overdose. I was only five years old. My mother found him in the basement, face down on the cold floor. I could hear her screams from outside in the front yard. I ran through the house looking for my mother and I found her cradling my father's lifeless body in her arms.

The people who used to give my mother money here and there to help her out with bills after my father died, were no longer supporters. The extra money stopped coming and my mother went broke. My mother's family wasn't much help because most of them didn't come around knowing she was involved with a drug dealer turned crack head. They never liked my father and damn near disowned my mother.

160

I pushed the thoughts of my past out of my mind and picked up my cell phone to call Moni. I blocked my number before calling. She didn't answer right away.

"Hello," she answered, sounding hesitant.

"Hey Moni! Happy birthday to you," I sung. "How does it feel to be twenty-one?"

"Hi KeKey, thank you, girl! It feels good." She sounded happy to hear from me. "How you doing? Everything alright?" she questioned. "You been on my mind hard lately."

I must admit I was smiling when she said she was thinking of me. Moni and I were best friends since we were little girls so I always felt really close to her. Hearing her voice made me miss her and home even more.

"Everything is straight. I missed you so much. I didn't think you wanted to hear from me though."

"Girl, p-lease! You do some wild shit but you still my sister."

Her words were so heart felt. I felt like I was getting soft because the emotions that filled my heart made me happy. I tried to play tough and wipe it off.

"Yeah we tight and all but I don't know about sisters." We laughed hard. "So what you and Rick doing for your birthday?" I was getting in her business like how she did me. "I know he doing something expensive and off the hook."

"Girl, I'm not with Rick anymore."

My mouth fell open. "When the fuck that happen? I thought ya'll were together forever."

"Yeah me too but too much was happening with him and I didn't have time for it. He gave me money to get a new house though. I can't wait til you come home to see it."

"What... he must really love you to give you dough even though you moving on."

"Yeah. He even knows about my new man," She told me happily.

"Get the fuck outta here!" What the fuck you do to Rick? That nigga don't be acting like that!"

"Now he does. He seems like he softening a little."

"Really? I gotta see this shit."

We stayed on the phone playing catch up for almost an hour. Moni sounded really happy with her new man. I could sense she had a lot of love for Rick too. I couldn't lie, the nigga did put it down like no other. He had women strung all over. I often thought back to how he had me coming like a flowing river.

After getting off the phone with Moni, Trent and I met up with this chick named Lily at Philadelphia Park. She was handling business for some dude name Roscoe. Apparently, Trent handled a lot of business for Roscoe over the years. He used to run coke for him but now Roscoe stepped down from the game. He still monitored the money but Lily and one of her brother's handled the drugs.

We were watching a horse race along with a huge crowd of people. I used to want a pony when I was little but I never realized how strong horses were. I would've been scared of their power. The race didn't start on time because one of the horses didn't wanna move out of the way of the race. It was four strong men trying to move the horse and he wouldn't move. Finally, some guy went to get some carrots for the horse to eat. The horse pretty much leaped off the racetrack after getting some food. Everyone who was watching was laughing.

When the race started, Lily approached us from the side. She was a short half black, half Latina. She almost looked like she could be related to Trent. She was thicker than me. I wore a size six. Lily was a size ten, a size bigger than Moni. She wore her hair long with her natural dark brown hair highlighted with honey blond. She definitely didn't look like she was into dealing drugs.

Trent leaned over to give her a hug and she smiled and started speaking Spanish.

"Usted pareciendo bebé bueno." She smiled at him.

I heard those words before when Trent would tell me how good I looked. *You looking good, baby* that's what she said. I knew she wasn't checking my man out in my face.

"Usted pareciendo bueno también."

You looking good, too that's what he said to her. I looked at both of them like they must have been fucking or still was fucking. Their bond was a little to close for me.

Trent introduced me to Lily and she all of a sudden started speaking English.

"Hey girl. Nice meeting you." She reached for my hand and shook it. "Trent must really like you. He never did the settling down thing." She laughed. Trent was looking at her like she better watch what she shared with me. "I'm pleased to meet you."

"Please to meet you too. How long have you known Trent?" I was all in her face.

"We went to school together. We go way back." She smiled.

That little bitch, I was thinking. I know this nigga did not bring me around some old high school fling he had. I made note to check him about that later.

"Oh that's cool," I lied.

After the first race was over, Trent insisted we go get a bite to eat. I felt like I was a sixth toe. I was out of place and I didn't fit into their conversation. I watched my man and his so called "home-girl from high school" chat it up the whole time we were at the restaurant. I wanted to be home with my own friends. Even though my mother was killed, I felt like she was still with me when I was home in Annapolis. In Philly, I felt like I lost her presence. Maybe it was because I lost myself when I moved to Philly. Maybe I lost myself way before Philly. Suddenly, I felt empty inside.

Chapter Twenty-Nine
Moni

Jay was walking towards the couch to make a last check of everything in his suitcase. He rolled his suitcase into the living room and then he paused in front the coffee table. My heart was racing something serious when I watched him looking at the panties that Rick ripped off of me. I was so mad at myself for allowing myself to lose control with Rick. I should've told him that I couldn't accept his gifts and sent him on his way. I couldn't though. It was something about gifts that made me feel extra special.

Jay turned towards me and looked at me with a weird stare. I was so nervous about what he was about to say so I started sweating on my forehead. I wiped my forehead with the back of my hand.

"Baby, what your panties doing on the floor?" he questioned. I was trying to make something come out of my mouth but I couldn't say a word. "Did you wash some clothes for our trip?"

Oh yeah, I didn't think about that. That sound like a good little white lie. I was so happy I didn't have to come up with something lame.

"Yeah, baby," I lied. "I must forgotten them when I was folding my clothes for the suitcase."

Jay bent over to pick the panties up and my heart jumped in my throat. I felt like I was choking. I patted my chest and I started coughing vigorously. Damn I would really be fucked trying to explain how my panties got ripped.

"Baby, you alright?" Jay rushed to my side and started softly patting my back. "What you chocking on, girl?"

I laughed but my thoughts were still on the damn panties. Jay joined me in laughter and I hurried to pick up the panties. I grabbed them out of his hands and it felt like a dark cloud lifted from over top of my head.

"I don't wanna forget these."

"It's a part of my sexy outfit I packed." I smiled seductively.

"Really baby?" Jay asked me. I nodded my head to agree. "Yeah, don't forget them. But it really would be hot if you pack some high heels and wear them with nothing else." He winked.

"I hear you, Mr. Nasty man." I blew a kiss to him.

I ran upstairs and put the panties in the back of my closet with the rest of my gifts. I took a deep breath and exhaled after being relieved from getting caught up right before our vacation.

I needed to think of a way to keep Jay away from the goods at least until the swelling went down. The constant thumping between my legs was like a reminder of the great sex I had with Rick. It was no denying how good it was. It was so good I wanted to pack my bags and move back home with Rick just so I could have that dick on a regular.

"Baby, you ready?" Jay interrupted my thoughts. "My brother gonna be here in ten minutes to take us to the airport."

"Oh ok. I didn't know you called him already."

"Yeah I did when you came upstairs. He can't wait to meet you." He smiled.

"Cool. I'm all ready." I smiled at the thought of meeting his brother.

I really wanted to push the guilty feelings aside. I didn't wanna ruin the surprise trip Jay had planned for us. He was doing everything possible to make sure I was happy and I was in there fucking around.

Jay would be so hurt if he found out what I did. I definitely planned to keep what we shared a secret. I smiled at Jay because I was happy with him but when I thought about the chemistry I still had with my ex, I knew I was in for some trouble.

Jay's brother, Aaron knocked at the door and we rushed downstairs to let him in. Jay opened the door for his brother and they hugged like they haven't seen each other for a long time. Of course that wasn't true. Jay's family was pretty close. His parents had dinner after church every Sunday.

"Hey, big brother," Jay embraced his brother.

"Hey, little brother. I see ya'll ready for this plane, huh?"

"Yeah, man. Come on in." Jay stepped back from the door and let his brother come into my house. "I want you to meet my lady, Monet." He stood by my side. "Monet, this is my brother that's four years older than me. But he shorter than me."

Aaron punched Jay in his arm. I flinched twice because the sound of that punch sounded like it hurt.

"Yeah you might be taller but I'm stronger, lil' brother."

Jay and his brother started talking about some fight that was on the other night. I enjoyed watching their brotherly connection. It made me miss my brothers.

"Let's get this show on the road," Aaron said.

Aaron and Jay carried our bags and I carried my purse and my neck pillow like I was carefree. It was nice having men waiting on me. I felt like royalty.

~~~~~~~~

It was a fast ride to the airport. When we got our suitcases, Jay finally told me where we were going. I kept pressing him to tell me where. I think I must have gotten on his nerves.

"Okay baby." Jay said. "You really wanna know where we going?"

"Yes, baby, tell me. Please!" I begged. He laughed. He then looked at me and grew silent before telling me where we were on our way to. "Come on, baby. Tell me."

"Okay. We are going to Miami." He announced like I had just won a trip on *The Price is Right*.

"Oh my God, Jay!" I leap into his arms. "I've always wanted to go there!" I was bouncing up and down in his arms.

"Damn girl, I like when you this excited." He buried his face in between my breast. "Keep 'em bouncing, baby!"

I hit him and then slid out of his arms.

"You a fool!" I started laughing.

Our flight to Miami was a little over three hours. We departed BWI a little after five and we arrived at MIA after eight p.m. The weather was so hot I started sweating right away. Although it was hot in Miami, it wasn't sticky hot like in Maryland. It was beautiful there. As soon as we got our suitcases, we headed over to the pickup area and awaiting a trolley to take us to get a rental car.

Jay booked a hotel right off of Miami Beach. When we went up to our room, I looked out our window and enjoyed the sexy beach bodies. I had to stop myself from drooling before Jay noticed what I was looking at. I loved Miami already.

Chapter Thirty
KeKey

I was feeling defeated when I didn't wanna join Trent to go back to Maryland. He practically begged and I refused. I was cool with standing my ground until lil' miss high school friend, Lily showed up at my door. I was walking around in Trent's t-shirt and she walked in after he opened the door. Trent gave her a hug and when they finished their sweet embrace, she turned to me.

"Hey, KeKey." She waved. "It's still not too late to get some clothes on to head to Maryland with us." She smiled.

"With us?" I questioned. I stared at her with piercing eyes. "I didn't know you were going." I stared at her and Trent trying to find out what the fuck was going on behind my back.

"Yeah mami, when Trent told me you weren't rolling with him, I told him I'd ride." Lily put her bags down at the door and walked past them. "What is that smell? It smells damn good in here!"

"That's breakfast. KeKey actually got the domestic thing down real good."

"Don't be putting that shit out there." I rolled my eyes. "You wanna a plate?" I looked at Lily.

"Hell yeah mami! What you got?" She asked while she followed me into the kitchen.

"I got fried potatoes, sausages, pancakes and eggs." I flashed a fake smile.

"Damn girl, what you pregnant?" she joked.

"No mami, Trent likes to eat *everything* up in here." I winked to Trent. "And I do mean everything." We shared a quick moment when I was flashing back to the night before and the way he put it down. "So you know I have to keep him well fed or he will eat somewhere else." I smiled.

"I hear that good shit."

"You wild, baby." Trent cut his eyes at me.

He knew damn well I wasn't feeling the idea of that bitch having breakfast with us. I was feeling a little jealous looking at her cleavage hang out of her low cut pink tank top she wore under a stylish jean jacket. As she walked they bounced. I looked at Trent who wasn't paying her any attention but if he wasn't looking then, he'd eventually get his peak in.

I fixed a plate of food for Lily. She sat next to Trent at the island. Trent was finished everything on his plate except for the pancakes. He was buttering them up and I grabbed the syrup from the stove top.

171

"You ready for some hot syrup, baby?" I handed him the syrup.

"Thanks babe." He winked. "This the best breakfast you ever fixed."

Trent and Lily both were digging into their food like a prison guard was gonna come at any moment to take their plates from them. I secretly hope she choked on her food. I smiled at the thought of her struggling for air. Trent broke my thoughts.

"Babe, you sure you not gon' roll with us?" He asked then he leaned back and adjusted his pants.

"I'm sure." I put my plate on the island across from him and sat down. "Ya'll can handle business without me."

"You been doing a lot of laying low lately. What you not feeling the game no more?"

Trent and Lily were staring at me, waiting for me to answer. I missed the money I got from doing jobs here and there but lately, I hadn't been going anywhere so I really didn't need to be paid like that. I had everything I needed in Trent's house and what I didn't have, I asked him to pick up for me. When I did leave out, it was very brief. I didn't wanna run into anyone nor have anyone talk to me.

I was getting so used to being in the house and not doing anything, I felt myself picking up a few pounds. I was cooking big meals everyday just to keep myself entertained. Each day, I was missing my mother, my sister, and my friends more. Trent created this little piece of heaven for me in Philly but it didn't compare to what I was missing at home.

"Ya'll seem to be handling business well enough without me. I don't need to be an extra." I stuff a half of sausage in my mouth that I cut. "Don't worry about me."

Trent walked over to me and smacked my thigh.

"Girl, if you keep cooking and eating, you gon' blow up!"

I smacked his hand and rolled my eyes. "Ain't nothing wrong with gaining a little weight." I gave him attitude. "Besides, no man wants a stick anyway."

"I know that's right!" Lily high fived me.

After Trent and Lily finished their food, Trent carried their bags to the car. She cleaned the island off and started cleaning the scraps off the plates. I grabbed the plates from her.

"You don't have to do that," I told her. I put the plates in the sink. "But you can tell me what's the deal with you and Trent. Do I sense some feelings between ya'll or is it just me over evaluating shit?" I put my hand on my hip.

"Mami, please." She laughed. "Me and Trent?" She laughed harder. "That's some funny shit. But to answer your question, we are really close but never had any feelings or never will. I have a man and he has you."

"That doesn't mean shit," I huffed. "Your attraction to another man doesn't have nothin' do with who you got at home. That's bullshit, for real." I got closer to her face.

"I'm sorry you feel that way, mami, but I don't get down like that." She stepped back from me.

We heard the door open. Right on time. Trent interrupted our potential girl fight. She looked at me like she could have kicked my ass but I wasn't backing down.

"I hope ya'll getting separate rooms when you get to Maryland," I spoke jealously.

"Of course we are." Trent laughed. "What would make you think differently?"

I didn't want Miss thang all up in my business so I walked into the bedroom. Trent was right on my heels.

"Baby, what's the deal with you? Why you tripping all of a sudden?"

I really didn't have motive for my allegations so I knew I was tripping. I was jealous of their closeness and also jealous they were both going to Maryland. I wanted to go with them but I knew I wouldn't go back to Philly alive.

"It's just that you about to leave me. Now you going with her." I pointed to the direction of the living room. "What I'm supposed to do while ya'll gone?"

"Baby, we only staying one night. I will call you when I get settled in."

"Okay." I put my head down and he lifted it up with his hand to kiss me.

"You won't even miss me. I'll be back so fast."

At that point, I was wondering if I was being a little too needy. I was acting like a baby putting my feelings out there to Trent. I didn't wanna seem like the house wife waiting on him to come home. I wanted to do something to take my mind off of him but I didn't know what.

~~~~~~~~

It was about six p.m. when I was awakened from my sleep. I was stretched out on the couch. I was watching a movie after eating two crab cakes sandwiches with a side of potato salad. My stomach was still tight when I went to check out the noise that woke me up. I let the blanket fall to the floor and I slowly walked over to the door. I peeked outside. As I got closer, I heard whispers. I stopped and thought *who the fuck found me all the way out this bitch*? I heard more whispers and then a knock at the door.

"Nigga, you sure this were she live at?" the man was looking around outside the door.

I didn't recognize the voice so I hurried into my room and grabbed my gun. My heart was beating swiftly and fear took over my body. I looked at the window in the living room and wondered if I would survive if I needed to jump out. There was another knock at the door. I was shaking.

"Who is it?"

"You don't know us but we're friends of Trent." The tall dark skin one said.

I cocked my gun and then opened the door before either of them could blink. I put the barrel to the fat one's forehead and pushed it hard.

"What the fuck ya'll bitches want?" I asked sternly, like there wasn't an ounce of fear in me.

"Oh shit!" the fat one yelled. "Baby girl, we really are friends with your man. He was supposed to pick something up from me this morning but he didn't make it so he asked me to drop it off to you."

"Step the fuck back." I wasn't playing. I kept the gun to his head. "Open that shit up," I told the tall one.

I was a little embarrassed when I saw the bags of coke inside of a big brown bag.

"Can we leave it with you?"

I put the gun down. "I'm sorry. I'm just a little protective."

"Fucking right," the fat one said. "I pissed my pants." They both laughed. "Tell Trent he can use you as a body guard." He let out a sigh.

I was relieved to know someone didn't track me down. I hoped Trent wouldn't be mad about me pulling a gun but I had to protect myself.

Chapter Thirty-One
Rick

My head was spinning so much. I thought the knocking in my head was from my hangover. When I realized I had passed out on the couch from my mixture of Hennessey and weed, I sat up and shook my head to regain focus of my spinning head. The knocking in my head grew louder. I put my palm up to my forehead but the knocking wouldn't stop.

I damn near shit myself when I saw my front door get kicked in. The first thing I saw was a gun so I thought it was the police. I reached into my back pocket and pulled out my nine and cocked it. I saw a man step over the door, which was laid out on the floor.

"Rick!" he yelled. "Nigga, you in here?" He looked in my direction and I started laughing my ass off. "What the fuck is funny, nigga?" Ace asked. "I thought your ass was dead in this bitch. I knocked on the damn door for almost twenty minutes." He put his gun in his back pocket.

"Nigga! I passed out on the fucking couch." I stood up. "I must have been tired or some shit."

Ace was trying to put the door back on the hinges and I walked over to help him. He looked like he was about to shed some tears when he didn't know what the deal was with me.

"I can't believe you were sleep and didn't hear me knocking like the police out here."

"Damn nigga. I'm glad it was you and not the fucking police kicking in my door."

"Fucking right." Ace patted me on the shoulder. "I'll take care of your door. I didn't know what the fuck was up." He looked relieved to see I was not dead.

"Yeah nigga, you owe me for this shit."

"I got you."

"Matter of fact, I need a better door. If you kicked that shit in, image what the police can do." I rubbed my chin. "I want something that it will take a whole army to get through. "

After Ace had the door steady to the frame, he made a call to have someone come to my house to put a new door on. I wasn't gonna leave my house with the door open so Ace poured us both a drink and stretched out on the couch.

After my door was fixed, Ace and I met up with some of the niggas who worked the corners. We met up at my mother's restaurant. Her spot was always jumping at night and on Sunday's after the church crowd.

My mother's spot was the best place to meet up to handle business. There were a lot of locals who came out to enjoy my mother's southern twist of soul food so we went unnoticeable when we went around back to the large office. I had the office laid out like a living room with a desk in the corner so my mother could handler her business. There was a large plasma TV mounted to the wall. There were three Lazy-boys that surrounded a round table so you could get your eat on while chilling in front the TV.

I bought my mother a nice sized house in Crownsville that she turned into a bed and breakfast for Mother's Day of 2005. She named it, *Your Momma's Place*. The food was so popular, people kept telling her she should expand and open a restaurant, which had the same name. My mother was making a lot of money off the bed and breakfast but she needed me to help her expand. She didn't have to ask. When she told me about her ideas, I fronted the money to make it happen.

My mother was my heart. She was the only woman besides Moni I could trust. When she first found out about my street job, she damn near disowned me. She put me out of her house. I started staying with any bitch that had they own spot. I remember my mother's words like she just said them. *Jumping from woman to woman gon' give you something you didn't bargain for.* She was right because I ended up with a scandalous, gold digging-baby momma. I bought my mother a new house to make her forgive me. She was concerned at first because she thought her house would be taken if I even got in trouble. I would do anything to protect my mother. I put everything I owned in my mother's name, even my truck and my house. I was protective of my mother so she never had to struggle or ask for anything, as long as I was still alive.

When Ace and I walked through the back door of mother's spot, I saw my mother walking into the office with two plates of food. Ace rushed to her side and held the door open for her.

"I got it, Ms. Sonya," he insisted.

"Oh thank you, baby." She smiled.

My mother was a young mother. She had me at the age of sixteen. It was a hard struggle after my father left her when I was two. She didn't want any more kids after that. My parents were high school sweethearts. They dated all four years of high school. After the two of them broke up, it made my mother bitter towards men and it took her almost twenty years later to let someone get close to her. It was around the time she put me out of the house that Maurice came into her life. I hated that nigga until I realized he would do anything for my mother. I had never seen her more happy. He helped out at the restaurant all the time. They had been married for ten years. I no longer looked at him as my stepdad, he was my father. Maurice was ten years older than my mother. He retired early from his government job that he had for twenty years. He was everything that my mother needed him to be at the restaurant. He cooked and managed the bills, but he was best at his BBQ ribs and chicken.

Ace took the plates from my mother and she began to straighten out her clothes. She was looking like a plus size Lena Horne. She was beautiful. Ace had a secret crush on her since we were little boys. He told me about it later when he was drunk. He always complimented my mother on how good she looked or how good she cooked. She blushed and carried on like some little young girl. I hated how he made her smile but I always brushed it off.

"Hey baby. What's going on with cha?" She kissed me on my cheek as she hugged me.

"Ain't nuffin', momma." I kissed her back. "You looking good."

My mother was always happy when she saw me. She was extra happy working at the restaurant.

"I know, baby." She did a little pose. "I look good for having a grown ass man for a son."

I watched Ace carry over some plates to Tony and Black. They were smiling and ready jump into their food.

"Lil niggas! What I tell ya'll 'bout having my mother bring ya'll food?" They looked at me with fear. "I don't wanna see this shit again."

"Leave them boys alone," my mother insisted. "They ain't hurting nothing. I told them I would fix them a plate."

I looked at them and they didn't say a word. They almost looked scared to touch their food.

"The food's right there, you might as well eat it," I claimed.

"What you want? The usual?" My mother asked me.

"Yes, please." I smiled at my mother. "Ace, what you want?" I turned to Ace's direction.

"Yeah, the usual man." He smiled like he couldn't wait for a plate.

As momma and I walked out of the office, two more of my employees showed up. Ray and Greg waved to let me know they showed up. They're always late. They were worst than any black woman I had ever known. Ray and Greg were cousins. They looked more like brothers but Greg was a little darker and shorter. Ray was tall with a light brown complexion. They both thought they were gangstas. I called them baby gangstas. I liked them most out of all the young niggas that worked for me. They had a way about handling business on the streets that gave them hood credibility.

"What up Rick? How you doing Ms. Sonya?" Greg smiled at my mother.

"Ain't shit." I leaned my head back a little. "It's 'bout time ya'll niggas got here."

"Everything's good." My mother waved. "Ya'll wanna plate?"

"Yes ma'am," Ray and Greg said in unison.

"What I tell ya'll about that ma'am stuff?" My mother laughed. "I'm younger than both ya'll mommas."

Ray and Greg went into the office and joined everybody else. My mother and I walked down the small hallway to walk through the kitchen. My mother grabbed four large plates and piled them up with food. She put twice baked sweet potatoes with butter and brown sugar on all four plates. She also gave us two pieces of cornbread, which were sweet enough to be a slice of cake. Then she put potato salad and string beans on all the plates and we waited for the meats to be done. When it was done, she put a rack of ribs on mine and Ace's plate. She put fried chicken on Ray's and Greg's plates. My mother went back to attending to her customers. She smiled and waved to her regular customers.

I grabbed up two waitresses to help me carry the food to the office. They both were whispering and giggling while I lead them down the hallway. Right before I got to the office, I saw a man standing in the corner next to the bathroom. When I got closer, he stood with his shoulders wide and then he looked at his watch.

"Hi ladies." He waved. "Rick, it's about time you came out of the kitchen." He smiled.

My heart was beating fast and my face was steaming hot. I was pissed off that this mafucka thought it was cool to come up in my mother's place of business. I should have killed that nigga. Everything would be straight if he was off the map.

"How may I help you Trent, or is it FBI Agent Banks right now? I never know what hat you wearing." I teased.

183

He laughed at me but I didn't see the humor. Trent was one sly ass nigga. I couldn't stand a fake mafucka like him. I wanted to break his neck. The girls were staring like they were scared some shit was 'bout to jump off.

"Ladies, please take the food into the office for me." I asked.

"Yes and tell the fellas I said what's up." Trent smiled.

I hated a nigga that stepped outta bounds. He didn't know where to cross the line. I was fucked up because I didn't know what else Trent knew about me. I didn't wanna end up behind bars but it was obvious he came to Maryland for something.

Chapter Thirty-Two
Moni

Miami had me feeling good. I didn't want our trip to end. We pretty much chilled on the beach for the rest of the day that we arrived. I was tired from swimming and flying. Jay still was full of energy. After he got out of the shower, I got in. When I got out, he was stretched across the bed naked with his hands behind his head. Damn I didn't know what I was gonna do to get out of fucking.

When I walked past the bed, Jay's dick jumped and stood straight up. I could still feel the swelling Rick put on me earlier in the day. I looked at Jay and wanted the dick but feared he could tell I already had some.

"Look what you did to my dick." He smiled, looking so damn sexy. "What you gon' do about it?"

"You want me to kiss it for you?" I licked my lips.

I knew Jay wouldn't be satisfied with just a head job. I was thinking maybe I could put the skills to work and suck him to sleep but he was like a twenty-one year old on Viagra. His dick stayed hard all night long.

Jay moved one of his hands from behind his head and rubbed his dick.

"Yeah baby, I want you suck all of this." He caressed himself and smiled a naughty grin. "Then I want you to sit on it."

My mind was racing. I stared at Jay's two inch width, ten inch long dick as he moved his hand up and down. I was trying not to let my body react to the thought of him filling the spot between my legs but my juices already started flowing and dripping down my thigh.

I let my bathing towel fall from around my body and held my breast in my hands. I walked over to the bed and joined Jay.

"Your wish is my command," I whispered.

"Bring that sexy ass over here." He told me.

I started putting the head skills to work and I was getting hornier from Jay's moans but he made me tense up when he move my leg so he could play with me while I sucked him off. I wasn't given him my best efforts because I was wondering if he could feel the swelling I'd been feeling all day. Jay stopped me from giving him head and he stopped finger fucking me. I looked up at him to see why he stopped me.

"Damn, that pussy dripping wet," "Bring it up here so I can taste it."

"Hold on baby. Don't you wanna come first?"

"No, I wanna make you come first. We got all night, baby." He motioned for me to come closer. "I'ma lick that pussy until you can't take no more."

That was the shit I loved hearing. My freak'em session with Rick had abruptly left my mind. Jay lived up to his word. He had me coming so much I felt drunk and weak. My body was in the highest level of satisfaction zone.

~~~~~~~~

That Saturday, we went to the beach to swim. Jay's body was something serious. He was hitting the gym on a regular to get cut up for the trip. I could barely keep a shirt on him. He was looking mighty tasty so I didn't mind him walking around half naked and building his confidence from all the admirers. Jay had on a pair of red swimming trunks by Calvin Klein. He was looking sexier than the Calvin Klein models. I watched a group of women checking out my man from a far. I was thinking, *yeah, bitches, he's mine*. Jay stepped out of the water looking like Tyson Beckford. The package he had in the front of his swim trunks look like he has an extra pair hiding down there.

After swimming, we laid on the beach. Jay and I took turns rubbing sun block lotion over each other's bodies. He was looking so good a few men started checking him out. I wanted to enjoy the sun before we went back to our hotel room. It was early in the afternoon when more people started coming out to the beach. Jay went to grab us some sodas while I got comfortable on the beach chairs. We stayed in the sun for about an hour and then we went back to our hotel room to sleep.

Jay wanted to take me out to dinner for my birthday so he booked reservations to Emeril's restaurant. It was such a long wait at the door but we finally got seated fifteen minutes after our reservations. The food was excellent. Jay ate all his food and some food off my plate. I was too full to get another bite into my mouth.

"So what's next?"

"Whatever you wanna do, baby? It's your birthday weekend."

"Okay. Well let's hit up Wet Willies. I've heard the spot was cool."

"Okay. Let's get changed first." Jay motioned for our waiter. "Can I get the check please?"

After paying a small fortune on dinner, we were excited to leave and take in the nightlife in Miami.

~~~~~~~~

I stepped into Wet Willies looking like a celebrity. I had on a mini jean skirt with a black low cut shirt and a pair of gold six inches high sandals. I had a gold handbag and a ton of gold bangles bracelets on my wrist. I wore a pair of gold dangly earrings that set off the bangles. I wore some shimmery body lotion from Victoria's Secret.

When I walked through the door, all heads turned and jaws dropped. All eyes were on me until Jay walked in behind me. All the couples admired us. I was sure the men wished it was them. The woman probably was thinking the same about Jay. It was a table close to the bar with a group of women. Some had wedding bands and a few didn't. The brave, married one scooted her chair back and then stood up. She walked right past me and approached Jay. She admired his body he was showing off in a light blue shirt and jeans. His arms were buff hanging out of his sleeves and his chest was showing through his shirt too.

"Damn, you fine as all out doors," she flirted. "I hope to see more of you during my vacation." She winked at Jay then ran her fingertips over his chest.

"Thank you for the compliment." Jay moved her hand. "But I'm with my lady." He smiled while pulling me close to him. "I hope you enjoy the rest of your vacation, miss."

"I would enjoy it a little more if I had some of that young, sexy body of yours."

By that time, I was about to beat the shit out of her. I got in her face and Jay stood between us. She walked back to her table and shared a laugh at my expense with her girls. I was fuming until Jay pulled me in his arms and gave me an award winning kiss. It was a good performance for the hating ass bitches and I enjoyed it so much I felt some moister between my thighs.

After sharing our kiss, we got a seat near the other side of the bar. I looked back at the table and motioned my lips, *bitch,* and then I turned around to my man. I wanted some drama to jump off. I wish my girl KeKey was with me because I would have talked more shit.

We took out two drinks each while sitting at our table. After knocking those drinks out, Jay got another one. He was feeling it so he started confessing his love for me again.

"Monet, did I tell you how much I love you?" He was tipsy.

"Yes baby, you do all the time." I smiled.

"Yeah. I do don't I?" He laughed. "That's cuz I really love you."

"I love you too." I put my hand on his. "Are you drunk, sexy?"

"No yet, beautiful." He finished his third drink and was about to sip from the forth one. "I'm almost there, though."

"I know. Don't get too drunk 'cause I don't wanna leave you in the car while I go hit up a club."

"Yeah ok. You not going to any club down here with out me. Not dressed like that anyway," he spoke sternly. "Ain't no nigga pressing up on my baby."

I had a quick flashback to Rick doing a lot more than pressing up on me. He was all up in his girl. He was fucking me like I was still his princess.

After we left Wet Willies, we walked up a block and partied at Fat Tuesday. Jay ordered a "*Call A Cab*" drink from the bar. He drank it so fast his head started spinning. We were dancing in the room with the pool table. Then a dude walked in with a drink in his hand.

"What it dew playboy?" He shook Jay's hand. "Where ya'll from?"

"We're from Maryland." Jay said proudly. I was dipping it low and dropping it like I knew I was gonna get some of Jay's dick that night. I held Jay's hand and started grinding on him real fast. "This my lady, Monet."

"Hey shawty!" He winked. "I'm big Nick."

Big wasn't a lie. He was about 320 pounds and 6'2. He was dressed nicely and carried himself with a lot of confidence. He had a little skinny half black, half white girl on his arm. Her name was Amanda. She was pretty but she didn't have the titties to fill out her very low cut shirt and her flat ass did nothing for her skirt that showed off the top of her thong. Her skirt was an inch under her ass. There was no playing pool for her.

Nick challenged Jay to a game of pool and he gladly accepted. Nick got us all a round of drinks and I sat next to Amanda who started talking my head off. Our night of partying came to a fast end. Jay had another drink and damn near passed out on the table. Nick helped him to our rental car and I ended up driving him back to the hotel. I was a little mad because I got no dick after the club.

Chapter Thirty-Three
Rick

My lawyer, Kyle Busch, hit me up to let me know the judge who had my case wanted to have a speedy trial. He was doing everything in his power to slow it down. At the least, I was looking at three years on lock and I wasn't tryna do that shit. I didn't wanna hear shit about any time. I'd do house arrest but not jail. I knew they wanted me off the streets but I had more to accomplish before letting the game go.

It's been a minute since I got a good night's sleep. My mind was steady racing. My mother invited me over to her house for Sunday's dinner. The less I had to do, the more I reflected on my life.

My stepfather and I sat in front of the TV watching old movies and talking about life. He reflected on his life back when he was younger than me. He told me how he used to run the streets hustling, too. He was kicking a lot of knowledge to me.

"You might feel all powerful because you can buy what you want and money isn't a thing but at the end of the day, that money doesn't keep you warm. It doesn't cook for you or tell you how much it loves you." He laughed. "At some point in your life, you have to decide when you ready walk away from this life. No woman or no jail will make you walk away. You gotta do it for yourself, young man."

He was speaking deep about where I might be if I didn't walk away then he started pointing out shit that hit close to home.

"You know that nice young lady you had not gon' want an old hustler. She needs a man that will put her first, not money. Did you think she would stand by your side forever?" He stared at me. "I know you like taking care of your woman and your mother but son, you can't do anything for either of them behind bars."

"I hear that shit you talking old man."

"You better do more than hear. You better live it." He smiled.

I acted like it was funny on the outside but I was hearing him loud and clear. I couldn't function without thinking about making more money. I couldn't picture my life without Moni. I damn sure knew jail wasn't an option. I rather die first. I did my small time as a juvenile but as a grown man, I couldn't do it.

I got a call from Ace and then I shook those fucked up thoughts out of my head. My mother was in the kitchen washing dishes. I walked in poured myself a shot of rum and then thanked my mother for dinner.

"No problem, baby. You know you always welcome here." I kissed her on her check and then gulped down the rum. I poured one more. "You about to leave?" my mother didn't want me to go.

"Yes. I gotta go take care of some business." I gulped down the rum.

"Okay," As if she didn't approve. "I keep praying that you leave them streets alone." She turned to face me. "But I'm done raising you. You gotta be a grown man and learn for yourself."

"Momma, I'm straight. Ain't nothing gon' happen to me so stop worrying."

I poured another shot and then gulped it down. I put the glass in the sink of soapy water. My mother washed it as I turned towards the vibration in my pocket. *Damn, Ace, shit ain't that important to keep blowing a nigga up* I thought. I dug into my pocket and pulled out my cell phone and saw that I had a text message from Moni. I started smiling. She was texting me to tell me her plane just landed safely at BWI.

I met up with Ace at my house. He did a run for me earlier and was bringing me the money back. He was sitting in his car waiting for me when I pulled up. He knew I hated waiting on money so that nigga was prompt. We walked into my house and he handed me a knot of money. I pulled the rubber band off the money and started counting.

"Damn, nigga, what they bought the whole stash?"

"Hell yeah, nigga!" Ace plopped down on my couch. "I told you them niggas wasn't playing. They trying move nothing less than an ounce. They trying make that money."

"Fucking right. They came to the right place, too. We gon' get this money from them niggas."

"I told you not to sleep on them didn't I?" Ace bragged.

"Yeah but you know I don't like fucking with new faces. But since you cool with them niggas, I went with it. I'm glad I did too!"

I counted forty thousand dollars across the coffee table. After I put it back in a pile, Ace grabbed it up and put it on the money counter for a more accurate count. He smiled handing me back the money.

"Exactly 40 Gs," he told me.

I took the money over to the machine and counted twenty thousand dollars and handed it to Ace. He was looking at me crazy. He didn't put his hand out to take the money.

"What's that for?"

"It's for you, nigga. Take this shit before I change my mind."

His face lit up and he accepted the money. I smiled because it was a good feeling seeing my nigga step up to the business like he did. Ace has been my nigga from the beginning so as long as I was getting this money, he didn't have shit to worry about.

"Damn nigga! What made you so fucking generous?"

"I gotta look out for you nigga. You make sure you putting some of this money away for a rainy day. You know I won't be making money like this forever."

Ace pulled out some weed and rolled it up. He cracked the blunt with his fingernails and then sealed it back together by licking the wrap. He pressed the seam to make sure the weed was secure inside the blunt.

"Nigga, you talking crazy. You always gon' have dough."

"I'm never gonna be a broke ass nigga but I won't have money like this forever."

"Yeah I feel you. That's why I opened that hair salon for my baby momma and now we both working on finishing our realtor certifications."

"Oh yeah! How that shit going?"

"My lady making serious money at the salon. She works like two or three days a week but she trust her workers to handle business while she gone. She doesn't really have to work at all because booth rent alone pays more than enough money to keep the place running."

"That's what's up, nigga. That's why I paid for Moni to have a good education. They shit will pay off big for her."

"Yeah, I see her every now and then looking like she still stunnin!"

"Yeah, my princess stays fresh don't she?"

Ace passed the blunt.

"Yeah she be doing her thing." Ace told me. I hit the blunt and passed it back. I was already feeling the effects since I drunk all that rum earlier. "You still got love for her don't you?" He asked.

"Fucking right. That's my heart." I admitted. Ace passed the blunt. "We gon' get back together soon."

"Oh yeah. Does she know this?" Ace almost looked like he wanted to laugh.

"Yeah, nigga. She still loves me. She just got tired of my shit. I understand that but when my shit get right, she'll be right back home." I passed the blunt. "Go ahead and knock it out. I'm done."

"What about that nigga Jay, she fucking with."

"That nigga just a temporary replacement. Trust me Ace, Moni will be back."

Ace chilled out for a minute until his baby momma started blowing up his cell. She didn't play when it came time for him to be home. She was on him like a watchdog. He loved that girl and she was cool as a fan. She talked the same shit about getting Ace to leave the game alone but she got two kids to feed so that fast money always looked good when the kids needed something.

I pulled my cell out of my pocket and got comfortable on my couch. I called Moni to see how she enjoyed her trip.

"Hey princess. You been on my mind since your birthday. How was the trip?"

"It was cool. I was thinking about you, too,"

"Oh yeah?" I smiled.

"Yes." She took a deep breath. "Look Rick, I'm with Jay and what happened between us

197

can't happen again. I'm sorry if I mislead you." She sounded like she was letting me down easy.

"You know it don't work like that for me, shawty. You know I don't listen to words so when you show me that you want me to step back, then I will."

"What you mean? I keep telling you its over."

"I heard that shit but you don't mean it." I laughed. "Lemme come over real quick for round two."

"Hell no, Rick!" She spoke louder. "Jay is here right now. Plus, I told you its over."

"Okay princess, but I don't believe you."

"Please believe it's over."

"Do he put you sleep like I do?" She didn't respond. "I know he don't. He don't even spoil you like I did."

"Rick, money don't have nothing to do with spoiling me. I saw more of your damn money then I saw you. Won't you ask how much time Jay put in and how he makes me feel like a grown ass woman and not a little girl waiting at home playing house for you." Then she hung up the phone.

That shit left me all fucked up. I kept replaying our last words with each other. Then I realized how much I really hurt Moni and how she outgrew me. She never raised her voice at me like that. Now she hanging up phones in my ear. I didn't see us ever coming to an end like how she saw it. I wanted her to be by my side and in my corner for life but she gave up on me and walked away.

Chapter Thirty-Four
Moni

It was the third day I called out of work because my body felt so weak. It was almost ninety degrees outside and I was in the house balled up underneath blankets. Jay kept stopping by to bring me soup and crackers. I couldn't keep either of them down.

When Jay got off work, he rushed over to bring me something to eat. I was lying in my bed with the covers over my head sleeping. I was awakened when I heard him put the tray down next to me.

"Monet," he called. "Are you asleep, baby?"

"Not anymore," I answered.

"Baby, you didn't get your food I left you this morning." I pulled the covers from over my head and sat up. I adjusted my eyes to the bright light that was coming through the blinds next to my bed. I felt like shit. "Damn, baby. You really look sick. You look like how I felt that night we were in Miami and I was throwing back drinks." He smiled.

"Oh damn. I look that bad?" I started laughing.

"No baby, you don't look bad." He kissed my cheek. "You should go see the doctor. Maybe they can give you some antibiotics to get rid of whatever you got."

"I will make an appointment if I don't feel better tomorrow. But I feel fine now. It's just after I eat, I start feeling sick all over again."

"I see. That's why you don't wanna eat anything."

"Yeah. It's crazy. I'm might have to call off again tomorrow. If I do, I'll have you pick up some work from the office. I don't want them thinking I'm at home chilling. I just came back from vacation, too, so I don't want anyone tripping."

"Baby, you have been back from vacation for more than two months. I'm sure they are not sweating you missing a few days."

"I guess you're right," I agreed.

My bosses were pretty cool when it came to sick days and vacations. My boss always told me to go home if he thought I wasn't looking too well. He didn't want me getting anyone else at the office sick.

Still, it was a week after I returned from vacation they gave me a big bonus and promotion. Although that was two months back, I didn't want them thinking I was slacking after letting my new job go to my head. I loved my new job. It was flexible and I didn't have to work directly under my boss. I still reported to him but I worked at my own pace unless he needed something handled ASAP.

Jay shared my soup with me but he ended up eating majority of it. It was homemade chicken soup his mother made for me but I didn't have a taste for it. I think I made my body not want any food. I lay in my bed in Jay's arms until we fell asleep.

~~~~~~~~

I woke up feeling fine. Jay had left some ginger ale and crackers next to my bed. My stomach felt like I'd been starving for days. I was having hunger pains and I felt light headed. Normally, I waited until after I showered to eat breakfast but I rushed downstairs to fix some food. At first, I grabbed a bowl of cereal but it didn't take the hunger away. I went into my refrigerator and grabbed a pack of turkey sausages, some eggs, and toast. I cooked enough food for two people and ate all of it.

I got dressed for work and headed out the door so that I could get caught up on some work I missed earlier in the week. I was taking interstate 97 to work when I started feeling queasy. I no longer felt like I had an upset stomach, I felt nauseous. I tried to pull over on the side of the road but I didn't make it. I threw up my breakfast all over the front of my dress and on my steering wheel.

I was so pissed off tears start streaming down my face. I pulled over and started throwing up again. *What the fuck?* I was thinking to myself. I went to the back of my car and pulled out a big t-shirt I had on when I went swimming the weekend before. I was happy to see it and my beach towel. Good thing I forgot to take it in the house. I walked around the side of my car and pulled the dress off and changed into a shirt. I wiped my car down with the towel and dumped the messy clothes in my trunk.

I got back in my car and I comprehended what the fuck was going on.

"Oh my God!" I yelled. "I can't be fucking pregnant."

I knew I wasn't supposed to talking to God while using profanity but I couldn't help it. I wanted to get out my car and start walking in traffic. I was thinking back to all the freak'em sessions I had with Jay and recalled all of them being with condoms. We did have that one that slipped off but he didn't come in me. He felt it come off and put it back on.

"Oh my fucking God!" I yelled.

Rick didn't use one when we had our freak'em session. What the fuck was I thinking? The dick was so good I didn't bother to stop him. My birthday weekend, the weekend Jay and I went to Miami. It was a little over two months ago. *It can't be true. I had my period last month,* I thought.

I looked down at my body and noticed no change in its shape. I was so shook up I couldn't even get the damn key in the ignition. I sat back and took a deep breath and reflected on the possibilities of me being knocked up by the ex. I started crying.

After I got myself together, I called my job to tell them I wasn't going to make into the office another day and that Jay was going to bring some files home to me. I started my car and made a mad dash to the nearest grocery store and brought three different brands of pregnancy tests. I took them home and peed on all of them. They all told me I was pregnant. I lay in my bed sick and crying until I cried myself to sleep.

I woke up in the afternoon and fixed something to eat. I accidentally touched my stomach when I was cooking and the thought of it getting bigger made me sick and mad all over again. While I was in the store, I knew I wasn't gonna keep anything down so I bought a lot of liquid soups and beverages.

At last, I was able to keep the soup down. I had so much liquid in my body I was in the bathroom every hour to release it. I stopped crying before Jay got off from work. He came home again with soup, crackers, and ginger ale. He came into the living room and sat the food on the coffee table.

"Hey baby. You look better." He kissed me on my forehead. "I told your job I'd give you some files but I left them in the car."

"Okay, thank you." I was still sad.

"Is everything ok?"

He was concerned.

"Yeah I'm ok." I covered my stomach with my arms just in case he saw the growth that I didn't see. "I already ate but I'll take something to drink."

"It's coming right up."

I didn't feel like telling Jay that I was pregnant but when I realized I left the boxes from the pregnancy test in the bathroom trash, I knew he was gonna find out sooner than later. I was too weak to even run upstairs to hide the trash. Jay came back from the kitchen with a cup of ice for my soda then he gave me a kiss.

"You alright?" He smiled.

"I'm ok."

"You wouldn't lie to me would you?" He laughed. "My mother says it sound like you might have a little more than a stomach virus."

"Really?" I laughed. "What she say?"

Jay started laughing and then there was a knock at the door. We both looked at each other to see if the other was expecting someone. Then they rang the doorbell.

"Who is?" I yelled.

I got off the couch and walked towards the door. They never answered me so I peeped out of the peep whole and discovered who my visitor was. I step from the door and unlocked it. It was my sister and my niece. I had forgotten I was supposed to be babysitting. I let them in and begin hugging and kissing them.

"You are just getting too big, little lady," I said to my niece, Hailey. She was laughing and then she went into her little pocket and handed me a little bracelet. I looked at it and then put it on. "Isn't this the hottest bracelet you ever seen?" I showed my sister.

"Mommy helped me make it," she bragged.

"Your mother is just the best!" I smiled.

"You still aren't feeling well?" Vicky gave me a hug.

"No, but I'm going to the doctor tomorrow."

"Okay. Let me know what they find out."

I turned looking for Jay and he was nowhere to be found. I wondered where he went. I helped my sister into the living room with my niece's things. Then, she turned around to shut the door and then we both were startled.

"Monet Harrison!" Jay yelled from the top of the steps. "Oh my God, girl!" He came running downstairs. "I knew it, baby. I knew it." He picked me up off the floor and started spinning me around.

"If you don't put me down, boy!" I already knew what he discovered.

"Did you tell your sister?" Jay was excited. I shook my head no. "Go ahead and tell her."

"Tell me what?" Vicky questioned.

"Monet is having my baby," Jay blurted out.

I damn near felt to the floor when I heard the words fly out of his mouth. I felt like my feet were stuck to the floor. I was nonresponsive. My sister and Jay shared the same excitement but I didn't. I was about to die inside. I stood there in silence. I couldn't smile or say thank you to my sister's well wishes. Vicky started hugging Jay and I. I worked up the strength to hug her back.

I thought I had at least a month before telling him about the pregnancy. After seeing how happy he was, I wanted to jump off a building. Jay and my sister were practically planning my baby's birth and all that good stuff that goes along with a new baby. I was looking like a deer caught in headlights.

My sister left to go on a date with her boyfriend, Kenneth. He called weeks ago to tell me he was going to ask her to marry him when he took her out to dinner. It was their second year anniversary of dating. At first, he wasn't the best father or boyfriend, but then he started growing a little more right along with his daughter. They had a brief break up when he was acting a fool but the more time he spent with his daughter, the more he started missing the whole family package. They still had some issues that they didn't agree on but they always worked it out.

I was standing at the door telling my sister to enjoy her date. I watched her get in her car and Jay was standing by my side.

"Baby, I can't believe we're having a baby." His smile was from ear to ear. "I don't know how this is possible though because we used condoms often. Well except for that time we slipped up but that was a long time ago and I know that wasn't the time of conception." He looked me in my eyes. "Right, baby?"

Somebody please shoot me now, I thought.

"I haven't had a doctor's appointment yet. It could be a false pregnancy that my body is going through. I've heard of those before. The test can be positive but you're really not pregnant."

I think I was trying to make myself believe that lie more than anything. Jay definitely didn't believe it. He was looking at me like the words I was speaking were irrational. I never felt so shitty. I cheated on my wonderful boyfriend and there was no doubt in my mind the baby belonged to Rick.

Chapter Thirty-Five
Moni

It was almost two weeks since Jay found out I was pregnant. I had an early morning doctor's appointment. Jay wanted to take off from work to go with me but I told him it wasn't the type of visit he thought it was. My doctor just wanted to see me to take an official pregnancy test and to talk to me about the results.

I was sitting in the doctor's office at Anne Arundel Medical Center waiting to be seen by my doctor. I almost fell to the damn floor when I heard my name called and I looked up to see Meka standing in the doorway waiting for me to follow her. She stood at the door and held it open for me. When she closed the door behind me she smiled at me.

"Hey Monet, it's been a long time."

My life felt like it was spinning out of control. Meka was Neshay's best friend. Neshay was Ace's girlfriend. They were real close. They were always together. They were closer than most sisters I knew.

"Hey Meka, I didn't know you worked here." I smiled nervously.

"Yeah girl. I started working here about a year ago."

"Oh okay. You don't do hair anymore?"

"Only on Saturdays. That's Shay's busiest days so I help out at her shop." Then she got professional. "So you believe you're pregnant?"

"Yes. I took several home tests but I wasn't sure if they were true or not."

"Those tests are pretty accurate. Are you ready to discuss this further with Dr. Levy?

"Yeah. How long will that take?" I wanted to hurry up to get the embarrassment of running into Meka like that over with.

"Not long at all. Dr. Levy is pretty quick. He is a straight to the point type of doctor." She smiled.

"That's great." I was a little relieved.

The doctor entered into the room and introduced himself to me. "Hello Ms. Harrison. I'm Dr. Levy." He shook my hand. "I understand your regular doctor referred you to me," he stated.

"Yes she did. She told me that I would really love you so here I am."

Meka left the room while Dr. Levy asked me about my last period and all that good stuff. I did feel a good comfort level with him but I wanted to kill the doctor when he confirmed that I was in fact pregnant.

Dr. Levy was pleased to know that I was going to keep my baby. He gave me a prescription for prenatal vitamins and some medicine that would help me with the nauseous feeling. The doctor left me in the room alone to get my thoughts together. About ten minutes later, I heard a knock at the door.

"Monet, its Meka. Can I come in?"

"Sure."

She opened the door and she was looking at me like she could tell I wasn't feeling the idea of being pregnant. She sat in the doctor's chair and she grabbed my hand.

"Girl, you look so scared." She smiled. "Everything will be ok. Trust me, so many women have gone through this. So wipe that sad look off your face and be happy you are able to have children." She looked into my eyes to look for a sign of some happiness. I didn't show it though. "You have no idea how many women come in here every day that have difficulties having children. This is definitely a blessing. Watch, you will see."

"Thank you Meka. I don't feel like being a mother is a bad thing but I didn't plan this so I'm not ready, right now. I have a lot going on so this right here put a halt in my goals," I shared, unhappily.

I knew my boyfriend was excited to be the father of my child but my ex was the real father. Rick would never let another man raise his child. The scary thing was, Rick would want me back in his life and Jay would want nothing to do with me. I wanted my future to be with Jay. Rick wasn't ready to be a father to my child. His focus was getting money, not being a family man.

I didn't know how Ace did it, he ran with Rick and handled the street business, but when it came to his kids and his girl, he was there. Maybe he would have to teach Rick how to do the same thing. Right now, Rick Jr. sees more money than his dad. He may spend four nights out of a month with him. Of course, his gold digging baby momma don't mind the money.

I already knew this baby would change a lot of lives but I didn't know how. I did know Jay would never trust me again. He probably would never talk to me again. I would more than likely be a single mother because Jay would leave me and Rick would be out making money as usual.

~~~~~~~~

When I got home Jay was already there. He was sitting in the living room waiting for me to come home. He ran to me when he heard me walk through the door.

"Baby, you told me you would call me once you got the results of the test when you left the doctor's office." He kissed my cheek. "Is everything okay?

"Yeah. I needed some time to think to myself. I wasn't ready for this so it's a lot to adjust to."

"It's ok baby. I understand." He kissed my hand. "You need me get you anything?"

"No I'm good, thank you." I hugged Jay. "I need to lay down. I feel really tired." I started stretching and yarning.

"Are you still having morning sickness? My mother said it won't last too much longer. It would depend on how far along you are."

"Oh my God, Jay! I can't believe you told your mother I'm pregnant!" I was yelling. "I thought we agreed to keep this a secret until we knew for sure."

"I'm sorry, baby. My mother was concerned about you." He hugged me. "Calm down Monet. Don't get all worked up."

I hugged him back. It wasn't that I was mad that Jay shared my news. I was more embarrassed because when his mother found out the baby didn't belong to her son, she would flip out.

"I don't want everyone getting excited this early in the pregnancy. You never know what might happen."

"Okay. I won't say another word." He stepped back. "I already told my brothers and my best friend. Your sister told her fiancé, too. So a lot of people already know."

Meka might be my nurse at the doctor's office, but she loved to share gossip with Neshay, so it would be no time before Rick heard about the pregnancy.

That was one bullet I was trying to dodge. I wasn't ready for that drama. I hadn't heard from Rick since I got home from Miami. Maybe he gave up on us. He might have moved on to someone new. I must admit, the thought of him moving on made me feel a little jealous.

I wondered if he still thought about me the way I thought about him. He was on my mind a lot lately. Even when I told him that I moved on I wanted to take it back. When he was calling to check on me, it made me feel like I still had a special place in his heart. Now that I hadn't heard from him, I felt like that place in his heart might have disappeared.

Chapter Thirty-Six
Rick

It was a week away from my court date and my life was fucked up. Busch was still working on getting the date changed, again. It was just a matter of time before I went before the judge. I felt the more time we had, the more my lawyer could make my defense stronger. I started laying low from the business like my lawyer advised. I felt empty without handling money or having drugs ran to and from this and that place.

Since I was giving Moni time to develop her relationship with that nigga Jay, I felt like I wasn't needed anymore. Ace ran the street business. Nobody found that bitch KeKey. I knew she set me up in Philly. She was the reason I had the court date coming up and I was facing possible time. I wanted to kill her personally but I promised myself to let someone else handle that bitch. She did so many people dirty, it didn't take much effort to find someone that wanted to kill her for a small price.

Ace was getting money and I let him keep a big profit. He stepped up to running the business. Every cut he brought to me, I saved it and put it in my mother's business bank account. Ace was saving a lot of dough, too. He finished his realtor license. He was working his ass off, getting a lot of money.

Ace bought a new house for his family and remodeled the house he bought for his mother. He was doing it up big but I could tell he was about to let the drugs go just as much as I was. He never came right out to say it but he stacking dough for a reason. I wasn't mad at the idea. You never heard of a nigga just retiring from the drug business. They either get murdered or get locked up for a long ass time.

Ace and I met up at my mother's restaurant to discuss business. He requested the meeting between the two of us. I thought it could be that he was ready walk away from the business sooner than I thought.

"Hey nigga, where you been hiding at?" Ace joked. He gave me a brotherly hug while we shared a laugh.

"Nigga, I ain't been hiding. You know where the fuck I be!" We laughed. "I've been chilling."

"Yeah I hear you nigga." We walked into my mother's office and sat down to handle business.

"So what's going on? Business still good?"

"Hell yeah. Business never been better," he bragged. "I really been chasing this money so you know how that goes. I don't stop when it comes to my money."

"I hear that good shit." I told him.

After Ace gave me the money. I counted it and then put it aside so my mother could take care of it. My mother came in the office with food for the both of us.

"I know ya'll hungry, right?" She came walking in smiling like always.

"Yeah we hungry, momma. Thank you for looking out for us."

I handed my mother the money I wanted her to deposit and took the plates and sat them down.

"Thank you, Ms. Sonya," Ace said. "You really know how to treat a young man."

"You know I do baby." My mother laughed at Ace's flirting.

My mother went back to handling her business and Ace and I started digging into our food like we hadn't eaten in days.

"Other than business, I did need to talk to you about something." Ace looked like it was some bad news he had to share.

"You decided to step down?" I thought out loud.

"Nah nigga, not that." He laughed. "I think I got a few more transactions to organize before calling it quits on the game."

"That's what's up my nigga." We laughed. "So what's the deal?"

"When the last time you talked to Moni?"

When he mentioned Moni I knew it was something serious. Ace only told me real shit. I was wondering if she had gone and married that nigga Jay. I couldn't shack the thought and it was fucking with me.

"It's been a minute. I'm giving her the space she asked for."

"Oh yeah. I hear she pregnant."

"What? That's bullshit. Moni can't be having that nigga baby," I yelled. "Damn, Ace. That shit is fucked up right there."

"Yeah. I didn't hear you talk about it so I knew you didn't hear. Are you ok?"

"I'm straight. I'm just blown right now." Of course the news was fucking with me more than the idea of her getting married. Having a baby was the closest connection between two people. A baby kept you linked together forever. Marriage was supposed to be the same connection but most marriages didn't seem to last like they used to. "Who told you that shit?"

"Shay told me. You know her best friend work at the doctor's office. Moni has been seeing the doctor there. She's about four months into the pregnancy.

I started calculating in my mind and thought about the last time we were together. It was around four months ago. It was her birthday weekend when we fucked.

"Nigga, you lying to me. Is this shit for real?"

"Yeah that shit is crazy, huh?" Ace shook his head.

"No nigga, it's not." I jumped out of the chair. "That's my baby Ace. Moni and I were fucking around and shit happened. Now, she pregnant." I started smiling. "I know that's my baby. Can you believe this shit?" I was excited about the pregnancy.

"Nigga, you sure? Don't get your hopes up about the baby before talking to Moni. I don't want you getting caught up in this shit."

"Ace, listen to me. Moni is pregnant with my seed. I have to talk to her and let her know I'll be there for her. I'll give all this shit up to get her back."

"What about the court date? You heard the lawyer. He said you will have to take some years for the charges. That's the least he can do for you."

"I'ma make that shit work out. Trust me."

Nothing was gonna stand in the way of me getting my princess back. She had to talk to me because she knew that wasn't Jay's baby. I wondered if she told him that he might not be the father. I couldn't wait to get my shit together. I was gonna have to go holler at my baby mother. I loved the sound of that.

Chapter Thirty-Six
Rick

It was a little after midnight when I was sitting in my room waiting for Moni to answer my phone call. I had been calling her all night since Ace told me she was pregnant. She forwarded at least five of my calls to voicemail. After about the sixth call, she answered and got a little bitchy attitude. I was mad but I told myself it was her hormone.

"Rick, please stop calling me. I told you I'm with Jay," she demanded.

"Oh yeah, well how long that nigga gon' keep you when he find out that's my baby?" She didn't say anything. She started crying and then I knew that she knew it was mine. "Let me hear you say it's my baby, Moni. You know it is."

"I don't know that," she lied.

"Yes you do. Why you sitting there lying?"

"I'm not lying. It's Jay's baby. We're together and we gonna raise the baby as a family." She was still crying.

"Moni baby, you don't have to do that. You know I'll be there for you. I'll do whatever you want. I promise."

"I told you it's not yours Rick." She hung up the phone.

Moni wouldn't answer any more of my calls. My mind was already fucked up and I couldn't sleep. I was tossing and turning thinking about how fucked up it would be if Moni denied me of my baby. Was I really that fucked up that she didn't want my own flesh and blood to be a part of me? She knew how good I was to my son. I was there for him all the time. His mother never had to ask for anything.

I finally got my eyes to shut when my cell phone started ringing.

"Moni?" I didn't bother looking at the caller ID.

"Nah, nigga, this Ace. Were you sleep?" He sounded worried.

"I was trying to but can't." I sat up in the bed. "Why nigga, what's wrong?"

"Shay not feeling well. The doctors think it's a tubal pregnancy. We been around the emergency room for over an hour."

"Oh shit nigga. I'm sorry to hear that. You need me do anything?"

"No but I was supposed to make a drop at two a.m. to them cats I've been telling you about. I know you said you didn't wanna get your hands dirty but somebody gotta get this money."

I thought about it and I knew it would give Moni more of a reason not to talk to me if she knew I was still handling business. I was so greedy I wanted to jump out of bed before we lost such a big connect. Then, I thought about little young nigga Greg.

"Did you call Greg? You know that nigga been trying move from his corner," I informed Ace.

"Oh yeah. You trust him like that?"

"Fucking right. He always on point with his money. Call that nigga up and get him take care of business. Then call me when you find out what the deal is."

"Alright nigga. Sorry yo! I'll be there next time."

"Don't be sorry. You don't need to be running shit this late anyway, stay with your family. I hope Shay get better soon."

Ace called me back when Greg let him know he would make the exchange. He had a suitcase full of coke he took down to this little spot where people did their fishing in the Chesapeake Bay. Ace told his connect to give Greg twenty bricks of coke. Once Greg spotted the nigga making the purchase, he sent Ace a text message. Ace then texted me to let me know what the deal was.

I must have gotten two hours of sleep when I got another phone call waking me out of my sleep. I didn't have time to answer when I heard Ace yelling in the phone.

"Nigga! Wake the fuck up," he yelled into the phone. "You not gon' believe what the fuck just went down." Ace's tone shook me.

"Everything good with Shay? What's going on?" I was concerned.

"Yeah she okay. She wasn't pregnant. She had some gallstones fucking with her."

"Oh shit, is she feeling better?"

"Yeah she home now but you won't believe what happened."

"Please tell me Greg didn't fuck up the coke connect." I was fuming hot when I was thinking about shit being all fucked up.

"No, nigga. He got locked up. It was a fucking set up. His girl just called me."

"Damn, nigga. Where he at, the detention center?"

"Yeah. I talked to Busch and he told me Feds were behind the shit."

"Let me fucking guess, that nigga Trent huh?"

"Yeah I wish you never trusted that nigga."

"I know. That bitch KeKey behind all this shit. She probably sitting back showing that fake nigga where we be at and how we handle business. I can't stand that bitch!"

My fucking head was spinning. That fake nigga Trent knew too much of my fucking business for it to be a damn coincidence. That was a lot of fucking coke to be handling over to the police. That shit set me back a lot of dough. Then, I didn't know how much I could trust Greg to say the shit was his. I knew Trent tried to tie it to me. He wanted my ass off the street ASAP!

Right after I got off the phone with Ace, my lawyer hit me up about Greg's case. He already put up money for his bail but he didn't trust him to take the full charge.

"I got the money to get Greg out, Rick, but I hate to see your money go down the drain if he skip his court case."

"I hear you Busch. How was he when you talked to him?"

"He was shook up and scared. He pretty much had a clean record. A little juvenile charges but nothing as an adult. He kept saying he wanted to go home and didn't wanna go near this shit again. So he might talk if the Feds offers something nice to him."

My head was fucked up. It was too much shit happening in that little bit of time. I wanted to close my eyes and never wake up again until I thought back to Moni and my seed she was carrying. Damn, how did shit get so fucked up?

After getting off the phone with Kyle Busch, I called Ace to let him know we possibility had a snitch on our hands.

"Damn nigga. I knew we shouldn't have let that nigga make the exchange. I feel responsible. That was supposed to be me making that shit happen." Ace sounded bad.

"Don't worry about this shit. I'll handle it."

"I can't leave my family Rick. I gotta step back before shit really hit the fan."

I didn't respond because I knew it was coming soon. I sat and thought about it. I wasn't mad because Ace had too much to lose if he got caught up in this drug business. He was the only nigga I could trust though. Everything was falling apart.

"You got enough money to walk away with?" I was concerned for his family.

"Yeah nigga I told you we were gonna be set." He laughed. "What about you. You holding on to the game or walking away?"

"I keep telling myself it's my time to walk away but the streets won't let me go. They keep calling me."

"Yeah I feel you nigga but if you Moni's baby's father, you know she not gon' be down for you running the streets. She a little different now. She like my wifey Shay, she want her nigga at home."

I didn't need to think twice about that because I knew it was the truth. I wasn't ready let the fast money go but I wanted my princess and my baby in my life.

After I got off the phone with Ace, I got out the bed and got dress. I wasn't sleeping good anyway so I decided to pay Moni a visit. I was burning up inside that she wouldn't talk to me. What gave her the right to ignore me like some little whack ass nigga?

When I got to Moni's house, her and that nigga Jay cars were parked in the driveway. I knew she had to be leaving out for work soon so I waited in my car for about fifteen minutes until I saw her heading out the door. I got out of my car. I admired how beautiful my princess looked with her pregnant belly. I wanted to go over and hug her until the door opened again. Jay came walking out the house. He looked at me like he saw a ghost.

"What the fuck this nigga doing here?"

She didn't respond. She looked like she was glued to the place she was in.

"Moni. I need to talk to you please," I begged. "Just for a second."

"Get the fuck away from here," Jay manned up. "What's it gon' take for you to see Monet is my lady?"

"Look nigga." I approached them. "I wasn't talking to you. This shit between me and Moni."

"Get the fuck outta here." Jay still didn't back down.

"Rick please!" Moni was pleading for me to go. "Why are you doing this to me?"

"You really wanna know?" I stared them both down. Moni was looking at me like *please don't say anything*. "I'll let you know for real."

"Please do 'cause I'm fucking tired of this nigga still hanging around and showing up where he doesn't need to be."

"That's how you feel nigga? Well tell me this? Did Moni tell you that baby in her belly is mine? Did she tell you that shit?" I stood back and watched him digest it. "She's under the assumption that you willing to raise this baby as your own. Is that shit true?"

Moni almost fell to the ground and I reached for her. She started swing at me and I grabbed her arms to calm her down.

"Jay, let me explain," she cried.

"Get the fuck away from me bitch!"

He snatched away from Moni.

I punched that nigga dead in his mouth for disrespecting my princess.

"Don't you ever call her out her name."

I waited for him to fight back but he didn't.

"I knew some shit was up between the two of you." Jay started to cry and Moni looked at me like she wanted to kill me.

"How could you do this to me, Rick? Why you hurt him like that?" Moni cried. "I love him."

That shit hurt to see her crying over a nigga that disrespected her. I watched Jay hurry to his car and then pulled off. Moni chased after him crying and begging him to listen to her. She was telling him how sorry she was and Jay never stopped the car. I went to Moni to hug her but she got in her car and drove away from me. She told me she never wanted to talk to me again.

Chapter Thirty-Seven
KeKey

I didn't know if Trent was purposely trying to blow my mind so that I would fall in love with him and never leave or if he was trying to make up for all the nights he had been missing in action. Our time spent together had gotten shorter each time but at least he showered me with gifts and money. Most importantly, he gave me bomb ass head!

I was sitting at the island in the kitchen watching the dinner I prepared for us get cold. Trent was three hours late and he didn't call or anything. I was so frustrated and feeling lonely. I had been planning this dinner all week. He knew about it a while ago. He told me he would be there. *Where the fuck is he?* I was thinking while tapping my fingers against the top of the island.

I grabbed a piece of cold fried chicken off my plate and sat inside the window seat in the living room. I sat there, watching the rain hit against the window and pulled a piece of chicken off the bone then put it in my mouth. I was so upset with Trent that I wanted to cry. He was constantly breaking promises but try to shake it off because it felt like he had too much control over me. He knew where I was every second but he started tripping if I questioned him. I was feeling like I had more feeling for him than what he had for me.

I walked back into the kitchen and put my bone in the trash and then heated up my plate of food in the microwave. I went back to the window seat and ate my food while the rain relaxed my frustrating mood. I finished my food and Trent still hadn't come over. I picked up my cell phone from the coffee table and saw that I had no missed calls. I was about to call Trent but I decided against it.

I was in a fucked up mood so I put the food away and then went into the bathroom to wash the rest of the make-up off my face. I put my hair in a ponytail and I went back to the living room. I curled up on the couch and watched TV. It didn't take long for me to doze off.

It was after midnight when Trent decided to come walking through the door. He was soaked from head to toe so his shirt was hugging his muscles. He was carrying a little bag and some roses. I rolled my eyes when I glanced his direction. I hope he didn't think a gift and some stank ass roses was gonna make me forgive him for standing me up.

"Hey." He closed the door behind him. "I know you pissed off but let me tell you about the shit I got into today." He gave me a kiss on my cheek.

"Don't fucking touch me." I got up and walked away from him. "I'm so tired of this bullshit, Trent. Can you at least keep one promise?" I yelled.

Trent handed me the roses and I smacked them out of his hand and then watched him step over them.

"That was real fucked up!" he snapped at me. "What the fuck is wrong with you?" he yelled. "I told you my day was fucked up. You don't know the shit I face when I hit these streets." He was pleading for me to understand. I heard all that shit before so I went into the bedroom. "KeKey," Trent called. "KeKey. I know you hear me," he yelled.

I didn't answer him. I went into my room and started grabbing shit to put in my suitcases. I was getting tired of Trent's shit. It was time for me to leave.

"What the fuck you doing?" Trent walked up behind me. "You always saying you leaving and you never do. So take that shit out of your suitcase and stop acting like a little kid."

"No you need to show me some fucking respect. You running game on me and you know it. Always out in the streets, yeah I heard that before."

Trent turned me around by my arm really fast and he pulled me by my hair to the side. My head leaned back and then he started kissing me roughly.

"You so fucking sexy when you mad." He kissed me again.

I didn't want to give into what I was feeling but I got horny then my body and mind wasn't on the same page anymore. My mind was telling me to get my shit and go home but my body was telling me to get some of that bomb ass tongue Trent had.

"Niggas like you make me sick." I rolled my eyes.

Trent ran his thick warm tongue all over the spots of my neck that got me super horny. I started moaning loudly. I couldn't control my body anymore. Trent stuck his tongue in my ear and started twirling it around sending chills all over.

"You like that shit?" he whispered.

"Fucking right."

He pushed me on the bed and ripped my clothes off me. "Damn girl, I love how thick your body got. I've been thinking about you all day."

I smiled as he lifted my legs to my chest and start sucking on my pussy like he was famished for me. The grip on my legs were tight but I quickly forgot after he made me squirt out a nut. I started moaning louder and yelling for him not to stop.

Trent lifted my sexually exhausted body to the edge of the bed and then my hands felt to the floor. My knees were still on the bed and Trent held on to me with his strong arms.

"Lift that ass up higher," he demanded.

I did as he said and he started fucking me hard doggy style. His pounding was so hard you could hear it over my loud moans.

"I love how wet you get baby." He squeezed my ass and then smacked it. "Tell me you missed this dick."

"You know I missed that dick Trent."

Trent pulled his dick out of me and then bust a nut on my ass. He slapped his dick against my ass until he got hard again.

"Turn around and suck this dick," he was blunt.

"Okay baby."

I sucked him so good, he made more faces than Jim Carey. After he came again. I got on top of the dick and rode him hard until I came.

"Don't stop baby. I want this nut right here." He bounced me up and down on the dick faster. "Oh shit! Oh yeah, baby. Uggh..." He released his nut and I collapsed on top of him.

It was something about the dick that made everything change. We lay in the bed with the covers barely covering our naked bodies. Trent pulled me into his arms and he kissed me on my forehead.

"You still leaving?"

"Yup!" I told him. He laughed. "Ain't shit funny, nigga."

"Yes it is. You know you be tripping and shit." He hugged me tight. "You know you ain't going no where." Trent got out of the bed. "You want something to drink?"

"Yeah and some of the fried chicken too." I giggled. "You hungry? Your plate is in the microwave."

"Oh yeah. I'ma heat that up real quick."

Trent come back with two plates of food and the gift bag he had in his hand when he came through the door.

"Thank you." I reached for my plate. "What's in the bag?" I smiled.

I knew it had to be jewelry from how small the bag was. Trent handed me the bag and I fished through it and moved the tissue paper aside. To my surprise, it wasn't jewelry. It was a knot of money in there. I pulled it out and showed it to him.

"What's this for?" I damn near knocked my food in the floor.

I started counting the money while Trent ate his food. He winked at me.

"It's something I made today. I told you I was out taking care of business baby. You know I keep my word." He licked his finger. "You always thinking I'm doing wrong but I'm just making money."

"I'm sorry baby." I put my plate down and the money down and I sat in his lap and kissed him passionately.

Trent always knew how to make me feel better. I still wasn't over his disappearing acts or his late night. It would be different if he went straight home and didn't tell me when he got in but he knew I'd blow his phone up so he came over when he said he would. To make matters worse, he only visited me two or three times a week. At first, he came over everyday. Now, I had to demand his attention. I felt like a prisoner living in an expensive environment with diamonds and the latest fashions. I really missed home.

Chapter Thirty-Eight
Moni

I damn near ran back into my house when I saw Rick getting out of his truck. I noticed it but I didn't pay any attention that Rick would be at my house that early in the morning. I was looking down at my rounding stomach that seemed to get bigger each day. When I hear the door to his truck close, I looked his direction and I damn near lost my balance. I felt weak like I was about to faint.

I knew it was no good way for telling Jay Rick was the baby's father but I thought I'd be able to discuss the issue rationally and not have to come to the tears and yelling. I wanted to hold him and make the pain go away that I saw cover his face when he learned the paternity of my baby. He looked mad enough to hit me.

I didn't grasp how anxious Rick was to be apart of the baby's life and mine. I didn't appreciate the hurt he caused between Jay and me. I knew he would never talk to me again and for that, I never wanted to speak to Rick again.

I was so through with Rick's bullshit I left my cell phone in the car when I went to work. I didn't want to talk to him. I didn't want to hear one of his bullshit excuses for him coming between Jay and myself. I wanted to go home and start the day all over again. I wanted to start over as far as my birthday week and a stopped the great sex we shared.

My feelings were torn because I had grown to love the little gift from God that was growing in my stomach but I hated the baby's father for what he had done to my future. Rick had made me a young mother and he had no plans of making me his wife. With Jay, he was talking about getting married so that the baby and I both could have his last name. Then I was having mixed feelings because I couldn't deny the feelings I had for Rick.

Even though my feelings for Rick were very strong, I knew he wasn't about being a family man. I sensed that he was only trying to be a part of the baby's life just to get back with me. My feelings were all mixed up and I was stressing way too much.

I got to my desk and I called Jay's office. When the receptionist picked up the phone, she greeted me. When I told her who I was and who I was calling for, she told me that he would be in a meeting all day. I didn't buy that bullshit because Jay always told me about all his upcoming meetings.

"Can you please tell him to give me a call when he's available?"

"I sure will," she lied.

I called back about five times before I realized there was no hope of talking to him. By the end of the week, Jay relocated to his company's Virginia office. When the receptionist gave me the news, I felt an emptiness in the pit of my stomach.

Gone to Virginia? I thought. *How could he leave without saying bye to me?*

~~~~~~~~~

It took me over three weeks to talk to Rick. I didn't feel anger towards him like I used to. Most of my anger was at myself for allowing myself to get in such a fucked up situation. I must have been a fool to think Jay would raise Rick's baby or for thinking Rick would let him.

"Moni, I'm happy you decided to take my call," Rick said. "When you told me it was ok to come over, I fucking ran out the door like police was chasing me." He laughed as he walked into my house.

"Yeah I couldn't stop speaking to you. I knew that wasn't realistic." I hugged him.

"That's good princess, 'cause I really missed you. I know I fucked up and I'm sorry but this shit right here happened for a reason." He rubbed my stomach. "We were supposed to be together." He paused as we walked towards the dinning room. "For real baby, every since I found out you were pregnant, I started changing my life." He chuckled. "I know it's hard to believe but I gave up the drugs, Moni. I did. I know you don't believe me but I did it all for you and my baby." We both sat down.

"Rick, you don't have to lie to me." I wasn't convinced. "I'm not asking anything of you just to be in the baby's life."

"I'm not lying. I swear on my mother that I stopped."

"What made you give it up? I can't picture you laying low from the business. So what are you doing?"

"I started helping my mother out with her business. All the money I made, I'm putting it to good use. I'm going to open a business that's help out under privileged kids. It's gonna be a non-profit joint."

"So where you gonna get money from to take care of your family?" I couldn't wait to hear his new get-right plan.

"That's just one of my businesses, baby. Trust me, I got shit planned out."

"What about Ace and the rest of the crew?"

"Ace stepped back too. He got his shit together for his family. Him and Shay got married and moved to the country."

"Oh yeah? That's off the hook!"

"Hell yeah. It was the best thing for that nigga though."

"What about you? You think you ready be a family man?"

"I'm more than ready shawty." He laughed. "I'm waiting on you to get your shit together." We both laughed.

"Oh okay. It's all on me."

"No for real, baby, I'm ready."

"What about the charges you facing in Philly?"

"I'm hoping they get drop but we will see. I understand if you wanna wait until after my court date and shit. That's cool."

"Wait for what?"

"To get married."

I damn near fell out my chair when I heard Rick say that.

"What the hell you want get married for? I don't know what happened to Rick but tell him I'm sitting here waiting to talk to him."

"Why you playing!" He smiled. "I'm serious. I want you to be my wife."

"I'm not marrying you because the baby is the only reason you wanna do shit right."

"That's part of it Moni, but I can't see you with no one else. You understand?" He hugged me and made me feel safe in his arms.

"So when is the court date?"

"Next month." He sighed. "Busch kept getting that shit extended but now, it's time to face the funk."

"You know Mr. Busch will look out for you."

"Yeah I know but fucking with the Feds is no joke, baby."

The rest of that evening I spent playing catch up about the baby and the shit Rick was going through with his charges and not sleeping. I did see a big improvement in him but I didn't know if it was a front to get me back so I decided to get a better feel for him before jumping into anything. I didn't want to put my feelings on the line and Rick started acting a fool all over again.

Chapter Thirty-Nine
Rick

Everything was going good in my life except for one thing. My court date was coming up. It was early November and Moni was seven months pregnant. We've been back together for almost three months. She stopped working a few weeks before because she was having difficulties with her blood pressure. Our little girl was putting a lot of pressure on her body so she had to take it easy.

Although she was supposed to be taking it easy, it didn't stop her from hitting up every baby store every chance she got. She spent more money on little pink stuff than I could make at the bar I opened up a month ago. The money was good and the bar stayed packed but Moni shopped like I was still hustling.

Money wasn't an issue. We both sold our houses and pocketed a lot of the money but we put a big chunk of it into getting a house that was recently built. It wasn't as big as the one I had but when Moni saw it, she fell in love with it. We decided to move to the eastern shore just to get away from the fast life in Annapolis. It was hard for me to not make some money when I got called but in our new home, it was no temptation of needing to have the latest ride. Many people on the shore didn't have the big flashy cars. The shore was definitely a good spot to start a family.

It was hard for Moni to trust me like she once did. I did so much fucking behind her back and I had to rebuild all those bridges I burnt. Every time I left out of the house, she had to know my every move. It was cool though, I kinda saw that coming.

Although I wasn't in the mix of things, I was still making money off the drug game. I couldn't completely step away until I had enough money stashed. The more I saved, the more Moni spent. I wanted my business to be successful but you had to put up money to make it.

Busch called me to tell me shit was going ok with the nigga Greg. He told him I'd give him a stash of money if he took the charge he was facing. The nigga manned up quickly. Greg's cousin Ray stepped up to the responsibility of handling business. He was still under me and Ace's wing but we made sure he did shit right. Ace still sat Ray up with our connects and he made sure Ray send money our way. At first I said I didn't want anything but it was my stash house he was running shit out of. It was my loyal connect I had developed over the years. Plus, I had a family to feed. Most of my connects wouldn't do business with Ray until I told them I approved the transactions.

I was trying to be strong and stay away from it but nigga wasn't trusting Ray and he called Ace. Since Ace told him he couldn't make the meeting. He demanded to get me on the phone. Once I talked to him and told him the changes we made to keep ourselves clean and out of shit, he was like he could respect that shit.

~~~~~~~~

My court date was on Monday, the 5th of November. Moni and I decided to make it a weekend trip to Philly. I didn't wanna be in Philly longer than necessary but Moni didn't trust me enough to make the trip by myself.

"Where we staying at again?" Moni was excited to see Philly.

We were about twenty minutes away from our hotel. When I did a lot of business, I left Moni at home. This trip meant a lot to her. She seemed like she could trust me more by being on my arm. She was proud to be seen with me again and showing of her pregnant belly.

"We staying at the Marriott in downtown Philly."

"Oh yeah, I remember. You said it was close to the court house right?" She adjusted her seat so her back could be comfortable.

"Yeah. I'm not looking forward to Monday." I told her.

I was getting nervous the more I thought about it.

"Everything gon' be straight, baby. Busch said he'd be up here Sunday night so he will let you know what's to be expected." She rubbed her hand on my shoulder. "You know he ain't gon' throw no surprises at you."

"Yeah you right." I reached over and rubbed her belly. "Is the baby sleep?" I smiled.

"No she wide awake. That's why I can't get comfortable in the car."

"I told you, you should have stayed home. You know this ride too long for you to be sitting straight up."

"I'm good, baby. I'll lay down in the back if I need to on the way home." She took my hand and kissed it. "I love you Rick." She smiled at me and I felt like nothing in the world mattered.

It didn't take much longer before we arrived at the hotel. Moni was tired by the time we got to our room. I rolled our luggage over by the huge king size bed we had. I took Moni by her hand and helped her into the bed.

"Won't you get some rest and then we can go take in Philly," I insisted.

"Okay baby. I was pumped up to be in Philly but now I'm too tired to move." Moni said.

"That's cool. I'll lay down with you for a little." I pulled the covers back and took off my belt and watch then set them on the nightstand next to the bed.

Moni was still sleeping when I woke up. I pulled out the hotel's directory to get some ideas of where we would eat dinner. I fingered through all the restaurants and decided to go with Cuba Libre. Moni never had Cuban food before so I knew she would love trying the spot I picked. She always liked trying new stuff. I was worried that with her pregnant hormones, she wouldn't enjoy the food.

After making reservations, I pulled out our dressy clothes from the dress bag that I hung up in the closet before taking a quick nap. I got Moni a black Olian maternity dress that tied in the front from Nordstrom. I hoped it fit well. She told me about the dress one day when she was shopping at the mall but she didn't get it because she thought she wouldn't have anywhere to wear it to. I took my black suit out the bag and laid it on the chair on top of Moni's dress.

I jumped in the shower while Moni was still sleeping. About ten minutes later, she joined me.

"That sleep felt good." She smiled. "You got room for me and my big ole belly?"

"Of course I do." I pulled the shower curtain back and helped her step into the tub.

She dropped the towel that she had around her body to the floor and I took in all her of her beauty.

"Thank you." She smiled.

She positioned her body under the water and I soaped up her cloth then washed her from head to toe. As the water rinsed the soap from her skin, I kissed her soft body and rubbed my hands all over her skin.

My touches lead us back to the bed where I bent her over the bed and ate her until she moaned and then started yelling my name.

I turned her over and gently made love to her whole body. I caressed her and told her how beautiful she was. Her eyes staring back at me made me think rationally, I was facing some time away from my beautiful princess and my kids. It was fucking with me inside but I didn't want Moni to start sharing the same fear. I held her tight and positioned myself inside her so I wouldn't squish the baby.

"Oh my God!" she yelled out. "That feels soooo good."

Moni held on to my arms and then she started kissing them softly as I continued stroking her. Her grip got tighter as she was coming. I lifted her legs in the air and I gave her long, deep dick until I came.

Chapter Forty
Moni

Rick and I were having dinner at this wonderful restaurant. He planned everything. He was excited to see I was enjoying the Cuban food. Since we were all dressed up, I wanted to hang out a little longer. We were going to drive around to find out what we got get into.

We were leaving the restaurant and Rick held the door open for me. He stopped in his tracks and I ended up walking into him.

"Rick, why did you stop?" I looked around him and saw what he was looking at.

"What's up, KeKey?" Rick asked.

KeKey eyes look like she saw a ghost. I was surprised to see her. She picked up some weight. She was closer to my size before I was pregnant. She didn't speak at first but I was so excited to see her, I pushed Rick to the side.

"Hi Rick," she said with no enthusiasm. "Oh my God! Moni." She reached out and rubbed my stomach. "Look at you all knocked up and stuff."

She laughed. "When are you due?" She pushed past Rick and gave me a big hug.

I knew she was surprised to see Rick and I together because the last time we talked, I told her that I was with Jay and Rick and I were history.

"We are due January first." I smiled. "On New Years."

"What the fuck you doing up in Philly?" Rick eyes were piercing.

"I moved up here with my boyfriend." She smiled. "He parking the car right now." She rolled her eyes at Rick. "So what ya'll doing in Philly? I thought I'd never see you again." She hugged me again.

"Rick had some business to take care of Monday."

"Yeah like she don't already fucking know! What you on the witness stand or some shit?"

"What? Know what?" KeKey was looking confused. "What the fuck you talking about?"

"Special Agent Banks," Rick said. "Funny running into you again without your badge and gun." Rick laughed. "What you coming to lock me up before the court hearing?"

KeKey was still standing there looking like she didn't know what was going on. She looked at Rick and then at Trent. Neither of them said anything.

"No Mr. Baker." He stood next to KeKey. "I'm about to have dinner with my lady." His smile was phony.

"What the fuck is the Special Agent Banks shit Trent?" KeKey was looking him up and down.

"You ain't know this nigga was Feds?" Rick laughed. "He sat my ass up when I came to Philly last time."

"Trent. Tell him he lying," she demanded. "Tell Rick he mistaking you for somebody else. You're last name isn't Banks. You're name is Trent Lopez right. Tell him." When Trent was standing there looking like a fool, KeKey started crying. She stepped back from him and she looked him up in down.

"You better speak the fuck up right now!" she yelled.

"KeKey, let's take this somewhere else," I said. The people crowding around us were embarrassing me.

"No Moni, because this bastard got some fucking explaining to do." Tears were pouring down her face.

"Tell her that good shit like you told me that night we met Trent." Rick smiled at him.

"Trent Banks is my real name, KeKey." He grabbed her hand. "I do work for the FBI."

KeKey snatched her hand from Trent and slapped the shit out of him. "Nigga, what the fuck you lying to me about shit like this for? What you were trying set me up too?" KeKey eyes were wide.

"That nigga married with kids and shit. How he gon' be your man?"

"Is that true, Trent?" She swallowed hard. "All of this was a fucking lie?" Trent didn't respond. "So is Lily your fucking wife?"

"No." He chuckled. "She's my lil sister."

"All this shit! Just one big ass lie!" KeKey yelled.

"No it wasn't. I really do love you. That wasn't part of the job but I still love you, KeKey." He told her.

KeKey pulled a small gun out of her purse and put it to Trent head.

"Nigga, you nothing but a fucking lie. You made me change my life for you. You made me get all fucking fat sitting at home waiting on your little dick having ass. I should fucking kill you for playing with me."

"Oh shit," Rick said. "KeKey, don't do this shit. You guaranteed to do life killing a Fed."

He reached out to grab her arm but she pulled back.

"I don't give a fuck. This nigga brained washed me. He took my life away from me."

KeKey got weak and put the gun down. Trent turned around and pulled the gun from her grip. He put the barrel in between her eyes.

"Bitch, you should have killed me when you had a chance." He cocked the gun. "I never loved your sorry ass. You were a piece of ass while I got to know all about who you ran with. Didn't you know this was a grown man's game?" He winked at her and then pushed the gun hard into her face and started laughing.

Police sirens were ringing loud as they approached us.

"We got get the fuck outta here Moni," Rick yelled.

"No. I can't leave KeKey like this."

I heard a car door slam.

"Give it up Banks. Let the young lady go," the officer said. "We got enough to prosecute her already."

Trent put the gun down and KeKey kicked him in his nuts. He dropped the gun on the ground and bent over in pain. KeKey bent over to pick up the gun and pointed it at the back of Trent's head. She didn't think twice before squeezing the trigger.

"No KeKey!" I yelled.

The police officer shot her in the leg so she fell to the ground and dropped her gun. KeKey started crying out in pain.

I wanted to go help her but Rick held me back. They put cuffs on KeKey and took her to jail. I was crying for her. I didn't know she was caught up in all that shit.

We went back to the hotel room and I couldn't sleep. Rick held me in his arms all night. I cried on his chest and he rocked me like a baby.

Epilogue

A year later...

Rick

Who would have ever thought the Feds were building a case on their dirty agent Banks. He had so much criminal activities the Feds were building against him. After a big drug bust, he started stealing money and drugs before it got to evidence.

The charges Banks built against me were thrown out of court thanks to the best lawyer. Busch's defense was the charges couldn't be credible from a dirty agent. Winning my case put enough money in his pockets. He could retire at thirty-five years old and live lovely.

After the birth of my daughter, Sonya Monet Baker, I decided it was time to put a ring on Moni's finger. She finally accepted. She became my wife February 14th 2008. It was about six weeks after she gave birth and she quickly went back to her original size. In March, I got full custody of my son so he moved in with us. Moni enjoyed him being there and he loved his little sister.

Our business was running smoothly. Moni pretty much ran the operations of the group home we started. I ran the business at the bar. My mother came by to make sure everything was going good. She even taught the cooks some of her recipes so we had some good ass food to serve while chilling at the bar.

Ace and I completely stepped back from the drug business. Ray took over and Greg was doing his time in jail. The judge only gave him three years so he took that with ease once he heard all the money I gave his mother for him once he got home.

I actually enjoyed working with the troubled teen boys at the group home. It took me a long ass time to get my shit straight. I wanted to lead them better then the leadership I had in my life. Not taking from my mother, but at some point she couldn't raise a grown man. Most of the troubled teens come from the same background as me. They were raised by single mothers and some raised by crack addicts.

Moni and my family were the reason I changed my life. I saw too much killing and I needed to get away from that life. My mother and stepfather got more involved in our lives. They helped out with the kids and we all went to church every Sunday together.

Moni

Funny how things change. Never would I think my best friend, KeKey was behind all the hang up phone calls and the robbery at the Mall. She confessed so much to me but I forgave her because she had a lot of years behind bars to think about all the ill shit she did to her friends and her family. I never understood why Rick hated her so much but that soon changed.

Of course Jay moved from Maryland and never looked back. He was making great money on his job and after he got over the hurt I caused him, he started a family with someone more deserving of his love. He still hadn't forgiven me but he moved on.

I was getting the kids ready for church after I fed them and got dressed. This was an important service for us. Rick was going to get baptized to have God wash all his sins away. I was so impressed with the changes Rick had made in his life.

Ms. Sonya was so proud of her son. They developed a stronger relationship once Rick stop running the streets. He put his family first and I never thought the day would come that I could say that.

I walked into the church with the baby in my arm and Rick Jr. was walking with his hand in his father's hand. Rick other hand was rubbing the small of my back.

We walked up to the third row of seats while waving to all the familiar faces. Even Ace and his family came out to see Rick's baptism. They sat next to us. They and hugged each other like it's been a very long time since they seen each other.

After the preacher gave a great service, she announced that the baptism was going to happen after the closing hymn. The choir stood to their feet, walked to the center of the pulpit, and then started singing *Blessed Assurance*. Everybody in the church was praising God and I reached over to Rick and grabbed his hand.

"Brother Rick, won't you join me up here," the pastor requested.

Rick walked up to the pulpit, stood next to the pastor and waved his hands back and forth while she started praying for him. When the choir finished the song, they went back to their seats and pastor and the deacon walked Rick over to the pool of water that was behind the pulpit.

The pastor and the deacon started praying for Rick together and they let him fall back into the water and then they brought him back up quickly.

"I pronounce you baptized in the name of the Father, the son, and the Holy Spirit," the pastor shouted into the microphone.

Rick gave her a hug and then he hugged the deacon. Ms. Sonya hugged me and then smiled at me. Silence fell over the church when we heard the doors open into the sanctuary. I turned back to see who was arriving to the service so late. My mouth fell open and my first reaction was to protect the babies.

I saw guns drawn from under some trench coats and then they started firing loudly. I saw Rick's body fall to the floor and everyone was crying and screaming. The gunmen ran out of the church and Ace jumped up.

"Stay with the kids," he yelled.

He ran to Rick's side. My heart was full of pain and I cried out once I realize what just took place in the house of God. How could this happen? Who could be so cruel?

There was so much crying and fear that come over the people in the church. I wanted to see if Rick was ok but his mother wouldn't let me leave her side. She cradled the children and me in her arms.

"Don't worry, Moni," she cried. "God will watch over my son."

Ms. Sonya had just as much fear in her eyes that I had. I held her tight while praying that God would spare my husband's life.

Now available:

Erotic Ink Publishing Presents:

Life Altering Love Addictions by
John Medley

Satisfied by Rukyyah J. Karreem

There's No Turning Back by
Rukyyah J. Karreem

Featured Anthologies:

That's the Way Love Goes
Tasty Temptations

Edited by Leila Jefferson
From
My Time Publications

www.eroticinkpublishing.com

Printed in the United States
210953BV00004B/4/P

9 780979 629716